CAIRO STORIES

Anne-Marie Drosso

Cairo Stories

TELEGRAM
London   San Francisco   Beirut

ISBN 10: 1-84659-025-6
ISBN 13: 978-1-84659-025-2

copyright © Anne-Marie Drosso 2007

This edition published 2007 by Telegram Books

A full CIP record for this book is available from the British Library
A full CIP record for this book is available from the Library of Congress

Manufactured in the United Kingdom by CPI

TELEGRAM
26 Westbourne Grove, London W2 5RH
825 Page Street, Suite 203, Berkeley, California 94710
Tabet Building, Mneimneh Street, Hamra, Beirut
www.telegrambooks.com

Contents

Voices

Ideal and dearly beloved voices
of those who are dead, or of those
who are lost to us like the dead.

Sometimes they speak to us in our dreams;
sometimes in thought the mind hears them.

And for a moment with their echo other echoes
return from the first poetry of our lives –
like music that extinguishes the far-off night.

CP Cavafy
from *The Complete Poems of Cavafy* (Harvard, 1976)

Twist

'Come on, let's twist again, like we did last summer ...' The girl, big for her age (she was turning eleven soon) had turned on the radio, almost full blast. Her father, far too old really to be her father, and perhaps for that reason much more indulgent than most, didn't seem to mind. In fact, the tune brought a half-smile to his face. Or was it the girl's vigorous twisting and turning to the music that cheered him up?

Studying her movements as best she could, in a long but narrow decorative mirror that hung in the living room, the girl had an idea. She could improve her twist by practising with the Hula-Hoop, which her mother had put away (she didn't want her using it in the apartment, for it could go flying and shatter pictures, lamps, mirrors, ceramic bowls, Chinese vases, glass ashtrays, silver jugs, Turkish trays or any number of knick-knacks – all objects to which the mother was far too attached, as far as the girl was concerned). A vase had been shattered in the past, and her mother, while restrained, had declared, with what sounded like absolute finality, that the Hula-Hoop was meant for the club and the club only, and was never to be used in the apartment.

The girl looked at her father, who was looking at her, and said, 'I think I'd dance much better if I could practice, just a little bit, with the Hula-Hoop. *Please*!'

'Just be careful,' he replied with evident complicity.

The mother was out for the evening. The old father and the little-but-big girl were on their own. They were both in the living room. The girl's schoolbooks and copybooks were scattered on a large table in the adjoining dining room – a mess that would have to be tidied up before the mother returned. The table was large enough to be used as a ping-pong table whenever the girl's friends visited. Lined up in the middle of the table, hardback books would serve as the net. Leather-bound books worked particularly well, but some of those were off-limits. The mother didn't seem to mind seeing the dining room transformed into a ping-pong room, as long as books she considered special were left alone. However, use of the Hula-Hoop at home she most definitely minded.

'Come on, let's twist again, like we did last summer ...' Humming the tune, the girl was now twisting with the Hula-Hoop around her. The summer was gone. It had been an unusually mild summer in Cairo and all of Egypt; the summer of her falling hopelessly in love with a fourteen-year old boy who had only a marginal interest in her. She had resigned herself to that but still thought about him and about what might have happened, had he reciprocated her love. He had held her hand twice at the club's open-air cinema. And had given her a kiss once. But that was all.

It was late fall now. The evenings were all of a sudden quite cool. Big, old Cairene apartments tend to be draughty and cold in the wintertime, requiring one to wear woollen sweaters. It hadn't quite reached that point yet, but the girl unexpectedly shivered. Her father noticed and was alarmed, 'Are you not feeling well?' he asked. 'You danced too strenuously. You ought to rest now, and then finish your homework.'

'I'm fine,' the girl replied impatiently. 'Besides, I've finished my homework.'

'But when? I didn't see you return to the table,' the father queried.

'When you were dozing,' she answered mischievously, knowing full well that he did not like to be reminded that he sometimes dozed in his armchair. On the coffee table right next to him there was a thick dictionary, as well as a tiny notepad and a pencil. While she did her homework in the evenings, he would bury his head in the dictionary, taking notes.

'I just closed my eyes for a few minutes. I was a bit tired. I had been reading for too long. You are old enough to know that when people close their eyes they're not necessarily asleep,' he said sternly.

Just as he finished saying this, they heard the click of a key in the front door. They quickly looked at each other. Could it be that her mother was back already? So soon? The girl jumped out of the Hula-Hoop, half-hid it behind the biggest of the upholstered arm-chairs, ran through the living room and the other sitting room, and saw her mother standing by the front door. The girl immediately noticed something unusual about the way her mother looked. She looked distracted, tentative, as if she wasn't entirely sure whether she belonged there, and whether she ought to step into the apart-ment. She didn't look at the girl, didn't acknowledge her.

'Mother,' the girl said shyly.

The father was heard asking from the living room, 'Is that you, Aida?'

The mother didn't answer. She stood still, the same vacant look on her face. A few seconds elapsed before she took what seemed like a reluctant step into the apartment, forgetting her key in the latch. The girl noticed the key, took it out and followed the mother, who was by now walking very slowly through the sitting room.

'Aida?' the father was heard saying once more, and again the mother said nothing but continued to walk as if on automatic pilot. Through the hallway, past the kitchen, then through the second hallway, and then straight into her bedroom. Without taking any of her clothes off, not even her jacket, and with her shoes still on, she first sat on her bed, then lay on it, clutching her purse in one hand and holding her forehead with the other.

She seemed to be looking at the ceiling.

For the first time, the girl noticed, really noticed, how high the ceilings were. And how intricate the work on their cornice was. She began counting the decorative indentations all along it.

'Where am I?' were the first words the mother uttered. 'Where?' she repeated.

Standing by the bedroom door, the girl looked stricken, yet managed to say, 'But at home, Mother, at home.'

'At home?' the mother repeated, almost inaudibly.

'Yes, in your bedroom, on your bed.' The girl was getting frightened. When would her mother start acting normal again? She heard her father's footsteps in the hallway and felt somewhat relieved but also nervous, for things were already complicated and she had a vague sense that his presence might complicate them even more. She couldn't have said exactly why she felt that way.

'Why are you in bed?' the father asked the mother as soon as he got into the room. 'What made you come back so much earlier than we expected?' He sounded solicitous and troubled.

The mother ignored his questions.

'What's wrong, Aida?' he asked, obviously bewildered. The girl, who was still holding the key which her mother had forgotten in the latch, exchanged a quick glance with her father, noticing that he seemed particularly old that evening, and that he also looked helpless. He looked like he could be her mother's father.

'Are you not feeling well?' he asked the mother. 'Perhaps a glass of water would help?'

'I do have a daughter, don't I? And she's away, isn't she?' There was complete silence in the room. And then the mother continued, 'And I have a sister, don't I? And she is away too, isn't she?' She was avoiding looking in the girl's, or in her husband's direction. So it appeared to the girl.

'Of course, you have a daughter who is in Europe right now, and one who is right here, by your side and, yes, your sister is in Europe, attending her daughter's wedding,' the father hastened to reply without quite managing to sound reassuring. He moved closer to the bed and put his hand on his wife's forehead, presumably to check her temperature and comfort her, just the way he did when the girl was sick.

The girl stepped backwards, almost but not quite into the hallway, wondering 'will she mention me now?'

The mother said nothing for a while. There was again utter silence in the room; the three of them appeared frozen in place. Then the mother said quizzically, 'So my niece is getting married.'

In saying that, she reminded the girl of a child who dutifully repeats a lesson.

'Do you want me to call the doctor?' the father asked. The mother didn't answer. She still seemed to be looking at the ceiling.

'I will call him. Right now,' he said eagerly, almost too eagerly, as though he was looking for the first opportunity to escape the room. He left abruptly, and could be heard rushing to the telephone.

The girl was left alone standing close to the door, looking at her mother, still wondering whether she would somehow acknowledge her presence.

'Does she not remember me?' The girl's heart started beating wildly. 'Does she not remember who I am? Why didn't she mention me? Why didn't she mention my father?'

Perhaps the mother wanted to forget them – both of them. Perhaps she wanted to live her life unencumbered, free from the two of them. Perhaps she ought to tell her mother, 'Mother, I'm here; I am your daughter. You know that, don't you?' But the words would not cross her lips. She could not make herself say them. To say them would be to acknowledge the possibility that her mother no longer knew her, no longer remembered her. To think that thought was one thing, to voice it was too much, so she kept still, waiting for her mother to revert to her old self – to stop being this stranger lying, fully clothed, on the bed.

It seemed like her father would never come back. She could hear him faintly. He was whispering on the phone, so he must have reached the doctor. Her mother had closed her eyes. The girl looked down. She'd been standing barefoot on the tiles and her feet were getting cold. She rubbed them against each other. 'Come on, let's twist again, like we did last summer …' The tune was back in her head. She found herself humming it softly. Then she thought she heard the call to prayer from the mosque she passed every time she walked to her aunt's place, but wasn't it too late in the evening for the prayer? Then the oddest question crossed her mind: would she still love her mother if her mother showed no signs of remembering her, or loving her? She might not; she might stop loving her.

She looked at her mother hard. Could it really be that she loved her only because she felt loved by her? Was this what that love was all about? What an intolerable thought! All of a sudden, the girl found herself running towards the bed where her mother lay. She knelt in front of it, laid her head on it, burying her face deep into the mattress. It didn't take long before she felt her mother's hand stroking her hair. 'Now she'll say my name,' the girl whispered to herself, 'now she will remember.'

Flight to Marsa Matruh

Around six in the evening, the holidaymakers would start gathering their belongings and amble back to their huts, hotel rooms and little villas to shower, have a nap, and plan outings meant to last late into the night. Often a few young men and women stayed behind on these long summer evenings, so the beach was never quite deserted. But it was rare for someone to be seen arriving at the beach then, except for parents shouting their children's names while surveying the shore and the sea, some nervously, others with exasperation.

Marsa Matruh's famed azure-coloured sea looked its most inviting just around that time of the evening, as the sun was about to set. Even the most prosaic of souls found themselves gripped by its shimmering surface. On their way back to their chalets and villas, men and women alike would turn round to look, one more time, at the expanse of blue, flowing into the rosy sky.

One such evening, Mrs Z., who had just arrived in Marsa Matruh intending to stay for only three days, turned up at the beach followed by a beach attendant, an adolescent carrying a folding chair. As they were approaching the sea, Mrs Z., though reserved by nature, found

herself, telling the young boy, 'Beautiful, isn't it?' With a propri-
etary air and beaming with pride the boy replied, 'This beach is the
most beautiful in the world.' Mrs Z. smiled. In one hand she held
a towel wrapped around a book and a swimming cap, and, in the
other, suntan lotion. Exceedingly fair, she had the type of skin that
burns easily. But to be carrying suntan lotion at that time of the day
seemed excessive: it indicated an overly cautious nature.

No longer young, she still had a marvellous face, without a
line or a frown – so symmetrical that those in search of exotica
might have found it boring, but for admirers of classical beauty,
it was a face to behold. An ivory complexion and very fine skin,
the straightest and most proportionate of noses, expressive lips
curling up at the corners as though hinting at a smile, honey-
coloured eyes highlighted by finely arched eyebrows – all this set
off by a perfectly oval face. Her wraparound beach dress, which
revealed little of her shape, hinted at modesty. She appeared to
be slim yet curvaceous. What betrayed a certain age were her soft
upper arms, and also, her hairdo, which was rather old-fashioned,
with locks of hair styled to curl around her cheeks.

When Mrs Z. pointed to a spot a few metres away from the
water, the young boy ran, unfolded the chair where she wanted it,
made sure it was steady and left whistling, satisfied with his tip.

Mrs Z. was not alone on the beach. A very young woman,
wearing white shorts and a white top – a girl really – was taunting
two young men by throwing balls of wet sand in their direction.
Pretending to retaliate with yet bigger ones, though not actually
throwing them, the young men visibly enjoyed the girl's taunts.
Her compact body moved like a cat, and she had a loud, sharp
laugh, surprisingly loud for a person of her size. From a distance,

she looked rather attractive, Mrs Z. thought, as she made herself comfortable in the folding chair, putting the book on her lap. 'A charming sight, as long as she does not throw her sand balls anywhere close,' was her next thought. A few seconds later, a sand ball landed at her feet.

'See what you've done!' one of the young men shouted. The girl ran to offer her apologies, which Mrs Z. accepted, saying 'I am unfortunately too old to take part in your games. Be careful next time,' to which the girl replied, 'You are not old at all; you look like a flower.' 'Come now, there is no need to resort to flattery. You've already apologised. Go and have fun with your friends. They're waiting for you,' Mrs Z. suggested. The girl burst out laughing and said, 'I must go home. They'll have to have fun without me.' Then she walked briskly towards a path leading to a cluster of chalets, ignoring the young men's entreaties for her to stay just a little longer.

Mrs Z. watched the shrinking, gazelle-like silhouette of the girl, who was now running. Watching her run, she became aware of a kind of longing – a longing for the freedom to do foolish and frivolous things. She could not remember a period, past her adolescence, when she had fully experienced that freedom. She had got married far too young, on an impulse. That was the worst part of it; she had only herself to blame. The marriage turned out to be thoroughly unsuitable. During the first ten years she had closed her eyes to its many shortcomings, not wanting to admit to herself, or others, that she had made a big mistake. When her pride subsided and she finally assessed the marriage for what it was, a failure, she had lacked the courage to end it and had soldiered on, barely keeping up appearances. It was a suffocating way to lead one's life.

'This is not a train of thought worth pursuing,' Mrs Z. admonished herself as she opened the book on her lap. A bit of reading, then a swim. Tomorrow, she would see her youngest daughter, who was at a holiday camp in Marsa Matruh. Though immensely glad to be seeing her daughter, she was anxious about the meeting, as she suspected that the little girl would beg her to take her back home. Some children love summer camp, others do not. Unlike her other children, her youngest daughter did not seem to like camp at all. How would she handle her daughter's pleas to go home – if it came to that? She hated having to use her authority to make people do what they did not want to do. It was not in her nature to control – or try to control – people's lives, even her children's lives. What would be the point of wrecking the little girl's summer by insisting that she stay in Marsa Matruh? Because camp is supposed to be a good experience for children to have? Because she herself was the kind of person who enjoyed group activities and interaction? These did not seem like good enough reasons. She feared that she might not have the heart to leave the girl in Marsa Matruh; and yet parenting was supposed to be, in part, about toughening one's children and, in the process, one's own heart. Tomorrow promised to bring a set of problems she did not feel up to facing.

For about half an hour, Mrs Z. immersed herself in her book; half an hour of pure pleasure. Then the book itself started another negative stream of thoughts with a passage that stated:

Life is not so simple. There are complications ... entanglements. It cuts all ways, till – till you don't know where you are.

She closed the book. It sounded like her life – cutting all ways 'till you don't know where you are'.

* * *

She had finally reached some fragile equilibrium in her marriage. Her husband had come to accept the attentions heaped upon her by her many admirers. His jealous outbursts were fewer and more short-lived. Not so long ago, in the course of a painful exchange, she had tried to explain to him that it was not love that tied her to the gentleman who had come to feature so heavily in her life. A certain affection, yes, and also gratitude for his attentions, but not love. While far from being a proponent of telling the truth at all times and at any cost, this time she had thought it important to let her husband know where she stood.

The gentleman himself she had done her best not to mislead. She had never told him that she loved him. She had offered him her friendship, and a little more, but, most of all, she had offered him a warm and understanding ear. Profoundly unhappy in his marriage, her lover was not as resigned to his unhappiness as she seemed to be to hers. She would listen to him express his anger at being tied to a marriage he had lost all interest in, and, as was typical of her, would counsel equanimity. Sometimes she even defended his wife. Her manner with him was always warm and serene, never demanding. In fact he wished that she would be more demanding of his time and attention, instead of just taking what he offered. He tried to convince himself that her reserve was because he was married, and, if he were free, she would be more demonstrative. But he sensed that the distance she maintained between them was insurmountable, that it reflected the way she felt about him. Whenever he had the courage to face up to that, he despaired, since she had come to symbolise for him a promise of happiness, however illusory. By listening to him as she did – with discernment, tact and without judgement – she had become his lifeline. They were both aware of that.

'And, so where am I at now?' Mrs Z. wondered, knowing the question to be silly and self-indulgent. She was in Marsa Matruh without her husband – and without Mr A. She was certain that her husband believed her to be in Marsa Matruh with Mr A. She had not disabused him of that idea, as she suspected that he would dread infinitely more the thought of her being there on her own than with Mr A., whose presence in her life he had come to tolerate to some extent. The knowledge that she was there on her own would lead him to imagine all sorts of things. He would be imagining that she might fall in love – really in love, this time.

So that was what it had come to: her husband finding Mr A.'s presence by her side reassuring, for he had chosen to believe her when she had revealed to him how she felt about the gentleman. It had not extinguished his jealousy, but it had tempered it. It occurred to her that, once back home, she would have to preserve her husband's impression that she had gone to Marsa Matruh with Mr A. – in a roundabout way of course since, when it came to such matters, she resorted to euphemisms to spare his pride.

Mr A. was not with her because she had wanted to be by herself in Marsa Matruh. It was as simple as that, but neither man would understand this. She recalled an awkward telephone conversation with Mr A., how she had been driven to tell him a white lie about her going. She had called to say that she would be going to check on how things were going for her little girl: 'Wonderful! I'll book a room at the Beau Site with full sea view. I'll say that I'm tied up with a business trip,' he declared enthusiastically.

She replied as firmly as she could: 'Well, I think it would be preferable for me to go by myself.'

'By yourself?' he exclaimed without giving her time to say anything else, and then, with a faltering voice, 'But why? Why?'

'To spend time with the little one.'

Sounding more upbeat, he countered, 'But you will have plenty of time. Mornings; afternoons; as you please. I'll be accommodating, you'll see.'

It was then that she felt compelled to tell her white lie: 'The truth is that my husband would take it very much to heart were he to find out that you came along, and that the little one found out about it. I don't want a big scene. I don't feel up to it. Besides, it's understandable that he'd get upset. The trip is meant to be for the little one. Surely you understand that?'

After a heavy silence, her lover proposed, with discernible diffidence, 'I may have a solution. What if I book myself a room in another hotel? Will that do?'

'I don't think so,' she replied. 'You know these resorts; it's hard to escape attention.'

'But to go by yourself makes no sense, no sense whatsoever when it would be so easy for us to be together!' he almost shouted.

'Be reasonable.' she replied, getting upset.

'I'm trying to be.' he said, so despondently that she briefly considered giving way but, in the end, stuck to her initial decision.

The conversation ended with his saying that he would book the room for her. Would she please allow him to do that? It would make him feel part of her little excursion.

She had let him make all the necessary arrangements, and, up until she left for Marsa Matruh, had had to endure his dejected tone whenever they spoke on the phone or met. It was clear that part of him was still hoping that she would change her mind and let him join her. He went so far as to write her a letter, complaining that she guarded her independence with such vigilance that it caused those who loved her to feel cut off from her. Would she forgive him for loving her as much as he did? The tone suggested that he might have guessed that she had used her husband as an excuse. She thanked him for the letter without referring to its contents.

In sum, she had used her husband to try to pacify her lover, and was using her lover to try to pacify her husband. That was where she was at – not a good place to be.

'Always equivocating', a friend once said affectionately of her at an intimate gathering where the guests were asked to describe each others' characters. And he had added, half-seriously, 'Here, even her smile is slightly equivocal', which had made people laugh. She too had laughed, as there was no doubt in her mind that the remarks were well-intentioned. Her friends liked her a lot – all of them did: that was unequivocal. She derived a great deal of comfort from that knowledge.

* * *

As Mrs Z.'s thoughts turned this way and that, the sun set and a small breeze could be felt. Years and years earlier, a man had made her appreciate nature and the outdoors in ways she had never experienced before, and never would experience after he ceased to be a part of her life. Him she had loved. She sighed a very small sigh. She was almost fifty years old, still made some men's hearts beat, was still the object of jealousy and desire and yet, instead of deriving pleasure from this, she felt it was all in vain. *Futility* was the title of the book resting on her lap – a title that seemed to capture her assessment of much of her life at this point in time.

There would be a dance at the hotel later in the evening; it was Saturday night. Mr A. had let her know – not too subtly – that he would mind her going to the dance. She had had no intention of going, although she rather enjoyed dancing, even if by her standards she wasn't too good at it. Yet she refused to promise him not to go. She did not want to give up the little bit of freedom she had carved for herself in a life she had come to experience as a web of confining ties and obligations and false gestures.

'Enough of these pointless thoughts,' she decided, getting up more energetically than was usual for her. She removed her dress, revealing an austere but flattering black swimsuit that provided a sharp contrast to her soft, fair skin. Adjusting her swimming cap, she walked towards the beach. When she reached the water she dipped her toes in, took a few steps, then, after standing still for a few seconds, walked in more resolutely and gently dived.

Mrs Z. was a methodical swimmer. Her favourite stroke was the crawl. From the way she swam it was evident that she was conscious of style and worked hard to do it right. Speed was not her objective. She was in fact quite a slow but tenacious swimmer, with a meticulous stroke despite her weak kicks. When on her own she stayed close to the shore. That evening she ventured reasonably far from the shore, and also swam for a long time – an hour or so – until it was almost dark.

Back on the beach, she looked around. The two young men, whose games with the girl had amused her, were gone. An older man walking with a stoop, his hands behind his back, was the only person to be seen, in addition to the young beach attendant who was playing with an abandoned, slightly deflated beach balloon. She had returned from her swim with the firm intent of taking her little girl back home, if the girl seemed miserable. She would not let her languish at camp.

At the intimate, old-fashioned hotel she was told by the receptionist that two telegrams were waiting for her. One from Mr A.: 'Am so tempted to join you – if only for a day. Call me at the office, if it is a "yes"!' and one from her husband: 'I hope that you and the little one are having a wonderful time. I miss you both!'

'I hope it's only good news,' the receptionist said.

'Yes, it's good news,' she answered, forcing herself to smile.

'Thank God!' he said.

'Thank God,' she repeated after him, then walked towards the stairs leading to her room, sorely tempted to crumple the pieces of paper in her hands and throw them away; she just crumpled them.

'Hilda, what a wonderful surprise!' she heard a man exclaim happily. It was a familiar voice. Could it be Max? It was, and just around the corner was Lola, his wife, equally happy to see her. They hugged and kissed. She was pleased to see them, welcoming any distraction. It so happened that she liked them – both of them. Max had once been rather in love with her, which had not stopped Lola from becoming a good friend over the years. There was not an ounce of jealousy between the two women.

'You must come to the dance,' Lola declared.

'I'm a bit tired,' she answered. 'Tomorrow I have to get up very early to have breakfast with the little one: she's not happy at camp.'

'Hilda, you must come; no ifs or buts; Rafiq will be there. He's on his own. I can't dance with both Max and Rafiq, so we definitely need you.'

'We do,' Max said, putting his arm around her shoulders.

Mrs Z. knew of Lola's soft spot for Rafiq. She smiled, 'I'll do my best.'

Lola replied, beaming, 'We count on you. Don't let us down.'

A petite woman, with average features, Lola had what people call sex appeal. It was the way she moved but also the way she flirted with everybody, men, women and children alike – a trait admired by Mrs Z., to whom flirting did not come easily. Lola's effervescence was catching. By the time she left them, Mrs Z. felt almost cheerful. 'What a fortuitous meeting,' she thought. Then, 'Why should I skip the dance? Why while away the evening by myself, moping about things that can't be changed?'

Once in her room she examined the clothes she had brought, noting the absence of a party dress; she had not planned on going out in the evening. However, she was not fussy about clothes, so that was not an issue. She put on a simple, straight black skirt which, like all her skirts, just covered her knees – a part of the female anatomy she found best hidden. And, to go with it, she chose a V-neck sweater made of very soft cotton – so soft it could pass for silk. Its rich green colour was especially becoming, as it highlighted her honey-coloured eyes. Black, high-heeled sandals with a fine strap gave the ensemble a dressy look. Just before leaving the room, she clasped a subdued necklace made of false pearls around her neck, quickly looked at herself in the mirror, judged the necklace to be appropriately understated, and hurried out of the room just as the phone rang.

The evening proved to be thoroughly enjoyable. The band was keen on the cha-cha-cha, a dance she danced well, though she did have to concentrate on the steps. She danced both with Max and with Rafiq. Not once did her mind wander to the subjects that had preoccupied her earlier in the evening. Even Max asking her, with solicitude, 'How are things going?' (he knew vaguely about the odd arrangements in her life) did not re-ignite her blue mood. She was determined to enjoy the evening. She answered Max's question with an evasive 'Quite alright.'

On her way back to her room, around midnight, she passed reception and heard the receptionist call, 'Madam'. There had been two phone calls for her. The gentleman handed her a folded piece of paper bearing the names of the callers. She put the piece of paper in her bag without bothering to unfold it.

In bed, she tried to read before going to sleep but couldn't concentrate. It was rare for her not to be able to concentrate. This whole situation had finally got on top of her. She could not help feeling she was betraying both men when, most of all, it was herself she was betraying. People assumed that she had always been the equivocating person she had become, accepting of all sorts of situations, open to any compromise. Yet, there was a time when she had been steadfast, daring, determined, even headstrong. Marrying the man she had married – in defiance of family and friends – attested to that.

She would write to both men tomorrow, telling them that the present situation could not go on. She had planned on an early-morning swim before going to see her daughter, but she would skip the swim and write those letters. Neither the marriage, nor the other relationship, made any sense. Neither was suitable. Neither was fulfilling. She began to compose the letters in her head, already dreading the consequences of sending them. Then, in the end, she fell asleep. But not soundly: every so often she woke up, tormented by the thought of how to explain to the two men, without hurting them too much, that she could no longer endure the present situation. But what was it exactly she could not endure? The tepidness of her own feelings? The constraints on her behaviour?

Very early in the morning, the phone rang. It was Mr A. – all apologetic. Yes, he had called her the previous evening, which was a foolish thing to do as she must have gone to the dance. It would have been a pity for her not to go. She deserved to have some fun. He was glad that she went, and felt immensely stupid for having suggested otherwise. Was the company pleasant, the band any good, the conversation interesting?

A few minutes after she put the receiver down the phone rang again. It was her husband. 'I hope that I am not disturbing you too early – but I wanted to remind you to treat the little one to an ice cream on my behalf. You know how much she loves ice creams! I'll let you go now. I know you're busy. Enjoy the rest of the weekend. It's dull here without you.'

* * *

The two phone calls revived Mrs Z.'s original plan to go for an early-morning swim. 'I must go for a swim, or I'll go mad,' she told herself, though she did not usually think in hyperbole. She hastily put on her swimsuit and wraparound beach dress, grabbed her swimming cap and was about to reach for the suntan lotion but changed her mind. It was not yet 7.30 in the morning. Besides, so what if a little bit of sun shone on her face!

Later, when she had calmed down in the water, words uttered by the man she had loved years earlier rang in her ears, 'It's touching to see you swim. You try so hard to do it right. It's so much like you; always trying hard to do it right.' Why had she lacked that sort of determination when it had come to their relationship? Why had she not followed her heart? She had no children then. Her excuses had been the difficulty of leaving a husband who had little but her left, and of upsetting the life of an ailing mother, whose fate was tied to hers – all in all, good, solid excuses. But, at bottom, something else had held her back, and it had nothing to do with selflessness, generosity of heart, guilt feelings, or filial devotion. She had loved the man and been loved in return, yet had been cursed with some ingrained scepticism about the permanence of such feelings. She had feared that the love would wane. This is what had immobilised her. In the end, it had seemed both cruel and senseless for her to be upsetting other people's lives – turning these lives upside down – for something that was likely to pass, namely, love. The day would come when her lover would be noticing other women, and she other men. And, even if that were not to happen, the day would come when they would take each other's love for granted, and show signs of tiring of each other. No amount of her doing it right would preserve their love the way she loved it.

This sense of foreboding had not been entirely speculative. One day, while discussing how to bring their lives together, he had seemed burdened by the complications involved. There had been a slight change in the tone of his voice of which he himself had been probably unaware. The change had not escaped her, giving her what she took to be a glimpse of the limits of his love. She had immediately felt her heart sinking and hardening. So she had slowly backed out of his life, letting him and the world think that family pressures had got the better of her.

Arriving at the beach, Mrs Z. set herself the target of swimming for a good forty-five minutes but, once in the water, she decided to take it easy. She turned on her back, letting herself float, the early-morning sun shining on her unprotected face. She tried to do some backstrokes but was, as always, hopeless at it.

It was time to return to the hotel. She would probably be late for the camp breakfast but, if she rushed, she might arrive before the end. She slowly swam back to the shore, making sure not to lift her head too high whenever she turned it sideways to take a breath. She wondered if the little one had made any progress mastering the crawl. Last time she had seen her swim, her strokes had been out of synch with her kicks. Was she really prepared to take the little one back home, if the girl begged her to? Now she was not so sure.

On the way to the hotel, she turned around to look at the sea. The splendour of the scenery – sky, sea and sand – left her feeling completely alone.

From Alexandria to Roseville

Paris checked his e-mail first thing that morning, and was surprised to find a message from Dr Jones.

The message read:

Dear Mr Dimitri,

I've just finished reading your father's extraordinary letter which, I gather, he must have given you not long after you had faxed me your notes. It would seem that you no longer need to see me. Should I cancel your appointment? If so, the fee would just be for the initial consultation. I'll be sending you a summary report based on the discussion we had, your notes and your father's letter.

If you think you still need to talk, I'll see you as scheduled on the 15th.

Having worked for over twenty years with old people, I must tell you that your father's circumstances and reaction stand out. By all means, if it at all appeals to you, accept his invitation.

Sincerely yours,

Dr Anthony Jones

Paris replied immediately:

Dear Dr Jones,

I would like to keep the appointment. While the crisis seems to have passed, I think I would benefit from one more consultation.

See you on the 15th.

Sincerely,

Paris

To his friend Peter, he wrote:

Peter,

I owe you many thanks for suggesting I contact your psychologist friend. It went well. I, who was initially reluctant to seek a professional opinion, am now insisting on seeing more of him!

Cheers,

Paris

P.S. How about a game of golf tomorrow afternoon?

Next, instead of looking at his other e-mails, Paris pulled out, from a file lying on top of his desk, the semi-autobiographical account he had written for Dr Jones, as well as his father's letter; he made himself comfortable and proceeded to re-read them.

* * *

Paris Notes for Dr Jones

Dear Dr Jones,

You suggested I jot down my thoughts about the situation and give you as much information about my father and myself as may be relevant. I spent a Sunday morning doing just that. I'm sure there is a stream-of-consciousness quality to my notes but I didn't think it necessary to edit them. It is probably best to let you sift through them yourself.

Sunny Homes is in Roseville, a twenty-minute drive from St Paul, where I live and work. It is the old people's home in which my seventy-two-year-old father now resides. It has a more homey feel than most old people's homes I've checked, but then I may not be entirely impartial since I chose it for him.

I grew up in Toronto, took a law degree in Montreal, then an MBA at Stanford and have been working for a publishing house in St Paul for just over five years. I am not married but have a partner – a social worker who lives in New York. We try to see each other at least twice a month. She comes to St Paul more often than I go to New York. Our friends wonder why. 'New York has so much more to offer,' they remark, more often than I care to hear. The fact is that I work long hours – often even on Saturdays. While Sharon also works hard, she's managed, thus far, to keep her weekends free. That's why mostly she comes to me. Besides, though outwardly calm, I really am an anxious traveller. I don't know how much longer Sharon will want to come and go, as often as she has been since we met at a friend's place in New York four years ago. Nor do I know what I'll do the day she decides that she has done her fair share of keeping the relationship going, and that it's now my turn. I want to think that I'll reciprocate, should it come to that. I'm very attached to her; we get along remarkably well. However, I'm set in my ways and tend to be compulsive about my work; thus, all in all, I am, I suppose, rather self-absorbed, as each one of my previous partners concluded after the first glow of our infatuation with each other had dimmed. Sharon may think so too, but has yet to say it.

As self-absorbed as I may be, the subject of my father's adjustment to Sunny Homes – or rather his failure to adjust to it – has been preying on my mind. It's only natural since he is my father, and I'm the one who suggested that he come to Roseville and move into that home – a move that required him to cross oceans; he came all the way from London, his place of residence for the previous twenty years. He has a combination of arthritis and gout that can be totally crippling and is the reason why I suggested he move to Sunny Homes, but, during periods of remission, he feels almost normal. He has sunk into a state of quasi-muteness since he moved to Sunny Homes two months ago. He'll say very little to me when I visit him. And the staff tell me that he says virtually nothing to them, and doesn't interact with the other residents. At the very outset – the first couple of days – he seemed willing to engage, then something snapped, and he stopped talking. He'll say 'thank you' and 'please', but no more than that. He spends his time either in his one-bedroom apartment or – if it's nice enough – smoking on the porch. He does go down to the dining-room for lunch and dinner (he usually skips breakfast) but looks so remote that none of the residents will sit with him. He went out once to check the Roseville library and never went back after that one time, though it isn't a bad library. It has much more than one would expect a library in Roseville to have. I thought that he would become one of its most assiduous users.

I suppose his case is not so unusual. An elderly gentleman, with sudden health problems, moves into an old people's home, in unfamiliar surroundings, and sinks into a blue funk. Still, I would never have anticipated that he would become so depressed that talking would get to be too much of an effort for him.

I tried to have him open up a bit and to draw him into a discussion of why he refuses to talk. Each time I tried, he smiled benignly and would not respond. Part of my problem is that I don't know him well. I don't know him the way a son normally knows his father. I have never lived, nor spent extended periods, with him. He and my mother were married for only a few months. They were already separated by the time I was born.

They met in the late sixties in Paris, where she was working for a publishing house. He was, by then, a successful translator of fiction and poetry, from Greek, Arabic and Russian into French, as well as into English; and from English into French, and French into English. I find it hard to believe that someone could master all these languages, three of which are very difficult. Occasionally, one hears of men and women who do, but they seem to be a thing of the past, to belong to a different era – like him, who was born in Egypt, in the mid-thirties.

Very soon after they were married – they married on the spur of the moment – my mother concluded that he was impossible to live with. He was, she used to tell me with obvious fondness, an incurable eccentric who balked at having any possessions, including cups, dishes, furniture, linen, even a bicycle, let alone a car. A true Spartan, living in and off books, with subjects of interest bordering on the obsessive, in which he would immerse himself to the exclusion of everything else. His ethereal nature had initially attracted her to him until she saw, she said, its flip-side – a lack of social know-how coupled with a disconcerting detachment; and yet, despite his apparent disinterest in personal interaction, he would astonish her by sometimes having flashes of insight about people and situations.

They remained friends after she had left him. Within two years of her leaving, she was working in New York where she met and married Greg, the man whom I would come to regard as my father, and with whom she moved to Toronto. Greg was Canadian, she American. As for my father, who lived, intermittently, in Paris, Athens, London, and New York, where he gained American citizenship, he always kept in touch with us. Perhaps he is not quite so detached a person as my mother portrayed him. But then, he may simply be a stickler for rituals. In any case, he would send us cards, send me birthday presents, would often call us, and over the years he stayed with us in Toronto several times. They were all short stays, even though Greg, who was fond of him, made him feel welcome, and the house in which we lived had ample room for visitors. My mother treated him with the sort of protective – slightly interfering – affection I expect sisters treat younger brothers; he did not seem to mind that, which I have always found hard to understand as he was, and still is, a very private man.

My first memory of him dates back to when I was around five years old – the memory of a man with spindly legs and a crop of bushy dark hair. Unlike Greg, who was of medium height and square, my father was tall and lanky. Paradoxically, I am built more like Greg than like him. My father still has a lot of hair, but it has gone all white, and he has developed a stoop so no longer seems so tall. I remember my mother telling me, before that first visit of his (the first I have a clear memory of), that I had two daddies, 'Daddy Greg' and 'Daddy Tony', so wasn't I a lucky child? Years later, she told me that I had sulked and muttered, 'I only want one daddy, Daddy Greg.' That part, I don't remember. I do remember, though, her telling me that it was up to me how I wanted to call 'Daddy Tony' and 'Daddy Greg', which smacked of pressuring me a bit into calling my father 'Daddy'. If subtle pressure was intended, it did not work. I made up my mind then and there not to call my father 'Dad' and stuck to my decision: Greg I would always call 'Dad'; my father I chose to call Tony. I still call him Tony, although, recently, I have found myself calling him 'Dad' a couple of times, feeling, afterwards, a tad disloyal towards Greg about that. Greg died of a heart attack a couple of years ago, and my mother of cancer five years earlier.

I believe that my father was quite content with my calling him Tony. In any case, he never showed any wish for me to call him 'Dad' or 'Daddy'. As a child, then as an adolescent, I got used to his distant presence in my life. I thought of him as a benevolent and somewhat peculiar uncle. For his part, he never tried to force himself into my life or demand any special marks of consideration from me, which was a relief, because I was very attached to Greg and did not want to seem to be changing allegiances.

Even when I was a little boy my father interacted with me as though I was an adult. That very first time I remember him visiting us he talked to me in a way that made my mother laugh and tell him, 'Hey Tony, the boy's not even in first grade.' It would take me a little while to get used to my father's English. Besides the fact that he used many words that were beyond a child's comprehension, he spoke English with a bit of an accent. It took me even longer to adjust to his social manner. He seemed either lost in thought and remote, or was, on the contrary, very present, commanding everybody's attention by firing off one idea after the next. He would talk mostly about ideas, hardly ever about anything concrete, tangible or personal, and he could get quite vehement. Much more vehement than any of the other adults who visited us, even though, unlike them, he never touched a drop of liquor. At first, his vehemence made me uneasy, even frightened. But then, observing that the other adults seemed to enjoy listening to him, I grew more comfortable with his style.

Once, he came to see us in the company of a woman, Maria. 'She is a staunch feminist,' he told my mother. In my early teens at the time of this visit, I was curious to see the woman for whom my father felt strongly enough to travel with. I did not know what to expect, as I had never seen him with a woman. Her being a staunch feminist heightened my curiosity. She turned out to be dainty and reserved. She was remarkably quiet throughout the weekend they spent with us. We never got to hear her views – feminist or otherwise. She was significantly younger than him, by then in his mid-forties. He seemed attentive to her every need as well as unsure of himself, unsure of how to behave in her presence. A day after they had been with us, I overheard my mother tell Greg, 'I sure hope it works. It's difficult for me to form an impression of her.' It did not work. We heard a few months later that Maria had decided that life with him was too austere. That was what he wrote on a card he sent us, adding in a post scriptum, 'Of course, she is right, but there's not much I can do about it!' My mother was upset for him. Greg suggested that he was perhaps happy on his own. 'He has no one,' my mother lamented, 'no brothers, no sisters, no father, no mother, no cousins he is in contact with. Just us, and we're miles away.'

Over the years, we paid him a few visits – once in New York, twice in Paris and twice in London. It did not matter where he lived, his place – always in the heart of the city – looked the same. A studio apartment littered with books and papers and with hardly any furniture to speak of. It is only relatively late in life that he acquired a computer and started collecting tapes and CDs, at which point he bought himself a rather fancy stereo system, after innumerable long distance telephone conversations with Greg about which kind to get.

Besides Maria, I never heard of another woman in his life, although he did have a couple of women friends who seemed quite fond of him. So my mother was not entirely correct when she said that he could count on no one but us. But, yes, he had no family and no partner, which is what prompted her to tell me, after she found out about her terminal cancer, to keep an eye on him; and to look after him the day he needed to be looked after. She wrote me a letter saying that. And told Greg to re-convey the message after she died.

My father was with us during the last days of my mother's life. I could not tell how he felt until the funeral when, all of a sudden, he seemed very distraught – he burst out sobbing – and Greg had to console him.

When Greg died, my father called me from London to say that he would not come to the service, that he would find it too hard. It is the one and only time he said something to me about his feelings. He was born in Alexandria in 1933. He spoke freely of his family background, but gave only the dry facts, never dwelling on what it had meant for him to have grown up in a world which, from all I heard about Alexandria of the thirties and forties, must have been a rather special place. Once, I tried to make him talk about that Alexandria, and he said, 'Paris [my mother thought that Greek name beautiful, and Paris was where she had met my father], what should I tell you? It's not as if I don't want to talk about it. But anything I can think of saying is trite. Should I be telling you that I loved to hang around the harbour and Ramleh Station, that I felt at home in the maze-like, seedy old Turkish Town, that, along parts of the Corniche, the smell of the sea and of fish could be overpowering; that the sunsets were beautiful; that many languages were spoken, often in a curious mishmash? All this has been said before by others much better than I could say it. And the truth is that, over the years, that part of my life – that world – has lost its reality for me. It has become a bit like a mirage. I can't feel it or smell it any longer. It's gone, very much gone. Some people look back. I'm not one of them.'

Of his Alexandrian origins, he told us that his father, a small grocery store owner, moved there in the early 1920s from a town in the Delta, where the grandfather had set up shop, using his teenage sons as helpers. I don't know how long the family had lived in that town before Tony's father moved to Alexandria at a time when apparently many Greek shopkeepers were leaving the Egyptian countryside and smaller towns. Hard times for cotton traders and their agents were hurting their business. They were hoping to do better in the big cities. Tony's father had always dreamed of living by the sea, and so chose to try his luck in Alexandria and, with borrowed money, he opened a tiny grocery store, renting an adjoining flat. The store and flat were in a poor part of the city. The father's only brother found himself a job in the canal industry, in Suez, and became a union organiser, which quickly became a subject of dissension between the two brothers, for Tony's father disliked unions. Another thorny subject between them was Tony's father marrying Tony's mother, a White Russian. The brother frowned upon that union; rarely did Greeks in Egypt, at the time, marry non-Greeks. The relationship between the two brothers worsened. That Tony's mother came from a solidly bourgeois background did not help. Her father had been a pharmacist in Kiev. She had fled Russia in her early twenties, going first to Istanbul, then to Alexandria. Tony was the couple's only child. His mother hardly ever set foot in the grocery store, of which he, however, has fond memories, perhaps, he said, because his father had never required him to work in it. His mother gave piano and French lessons and did embroidery piecework. 'Serious' is how Tony described her, whereas his father, he told us, had been a bubbly sort. When his father died of a heart attack and Tony was in his early teens, his mother sold the store and would have nothing to do with her brother-in-law, fearing that he would try to claim some sort of guardianship over Tony. She need not have worried, for the uncle left mother and son in peace. Luckily, she found a supervisory job in an embroidery workshop and managed to support herself and her son. Tony's life was not turned upside down by his father's death. Even though she sold the store, his mother kept the adjoining apartment, which remained their home. And he continued to attend the same Greek school – a school funded by the Greek community. When it became obvious that he had a special gift for languages, a rich benefactor (one of the co-owners of the embroidery workshop) offered to put him through university abroad. It was the early fifties. He went to Paris, where his mother had some distant relatives with whom he could stay for a while. A year later, his mother followed him to Paris. He lived with one set of her relatives, and she with another. Less than a year after her arrival, she died of a stroke. He had just turned twenty. He never went back to Egypt. His uncle left Egypt in the late fifties and emigrated to Australia.

After I graduated from law school, my mother and Greg, who, for some time, had been wanting to travel to Egypt, asked me whether I cared to go with them. My mother said she hoped I would, since after all, part of my origins lay in Egypt. They invited Tony to join us, but he declined. The fact that they had decided not to travel with a tour group did not sway him. He had no interest in revisiting the past, he told them. At the time, I had a girlfriend who was keen on Egyptology. So off we went to Egypt, the four of us. We went to Cairo, did the Nile cruise to Luxor and Aswan – the highlight of the trip – and spent two days in Alexandria. I liked what I saw of Egypt. Its people have a good sense of humour. In a curious way, Cairo reminded me of New York though I have yet to meet someone who agrees with me. I have been told that Cairo evokes Paris or Rome, as many of its downtown buildings were built by French and Italian architects. The city may well have resembled Paris or Rome in the past; I do not see the resemblance now.

Did I feel at all connected to Egypt? No, I felt no connection to it, which disappointed my mother, who had imagined me succumbing to some ancestral pull. There was a naive, idealist side to my mother that could either charm, or, irritate and drive one to take the opposite viewpoint. Still, I don't think I was suppressing feelings just for the sake of being contrary. No emotions surfaced.

It so happens that our whirlwind visit to Alexandria coincided with one of the Muslim feasts – the one when sheep get slaughtered, and those who can afford it give meat to those in need. The historical sites and museums were closed. All we did was wander through the city and walk along the sea, alongside large crowds of festive-looking strollers, many of whom – particularly children, teenagers but also young adults – hailed us with loud greetings: if it was not 'Hello!' it was 'Welcome to Egypt!' or 'How are you?' I gathered that our well-wishers couldn't speak much English beyond that.

Our guide in Cairo had recommended to us a fish restaurant catering to an Egyptian clientele – not a tourists' haunt. At the end of our first day of roaming through the city, we set about finding it, wondering whether it would be open during a feast when the tradition is to eat red meat. The directions we had were very sketchy but we found it, and it was open, and we had a superb dinner that evening. We miraculously stumbled on the restaurant, after a long walk from a fort that lies at one end of the western side of the Corniche – a walk through a maze of streets and alleys in what was clearly a poorer part of Alexandria. It might even have been the neighbourhood in which Tony had grown up. We didn't have the name of his street. He had told us that the name had changed, and he didn't know its new name.

Over dinner, Greg raised the inevitable subject of Alexandria's cosmopolitan past. The four of us agreed that Cairo seems more cosmopolitan than Alexandria, so things must have changed a great deal since the days when Alexandria had the reputation of being the more cosmopolitan city. But what does 'cosmopolitan' really mean with reference to a city, my mother then asked. Durrell's world may have been cosmopolitan, but what about the world of the poorer Greeks (the world in which Tony had grown up), the poorer Italians, Muslim, Coptic and Jewish Egyptians? Had their world been cosmopolitan? Like all discussions in which people talk about what they hardly know, ours went round in circles, until we all concluded that it would have been great to have had Tony participate in the discussion, though I somehow doubt that he would have.

So what made me think that a man who had grown up in cosmopolitan Alexandria (whatever that term means) and had lived in New York and big European cities would, at the end of his life, adjust to an old people's home in Roseville, Minnesota? What was I thinking? I suppose I took it for granted that he was an adaptable sort, whose anchor was his work and intellectual pursuits, for whom externals did not matter so much, a man used to moving from place to place, who could give meaning to his life between the four walls of any room. In any world. For whom language would not be a problem in Roseville. Because of his Spartan ways, his solitary nature, his being internally motivated, I thought that he would be fine, wherever he was, as long as he had books and work to do (he still does translation work).

Evidently, I was very wrong. So what do I do now? Frankly, were he to give me any indications that he wants to return to London, I wouldn't stand in his way. I would even offer to organise his getting re-established there, though I worry that he might remain depressed, once there.

* * *

Tony's Letter to Paris

Paris,

My withdrawing into a shell must have been very hard on you. I owe you an explanation.

For the last couple of months, I've been waking up every day around four in the morning and, more often than not, cannot go back to sleep. I toss and turn in bed, thinking that, since sleep eludes me, I should get up and read, or work on some translation but, instead, I lie awake in bed – till seven, eight, or even as late as nine – beset by the same questions: should I be going back to London? And, could I manage on my own there? Today, rather than just feeling overwhelmed by the questions and the prospect of having to make a decision, I managed to think through some of the practical implications of going back – and decided that it might well be the thing to do, if only because I miss the hubbub of city life.

It's curious that I should have reached that conclusion today, for, just yesterday, life here stopped feeling as bleak as it had been feeling. Yesterday was the first day since I have been here that I've been in the mood to do something. In fact, two things: play chess and learn sign language. While smoking on the porch in the late afternoon, I saw two men play a game of chess, pulled my chair next to them, and watched them play. They did not seem to mind; nor did they seem to mind my smoking. They were playing in utter silence. It took me a while before I realised that one of them was completely deaf. Both were good players – equally good, although the deaf gentleman was more daring. He made, by far, the bolder moves and had an unusual strategy that immediately grabbed my interest. Unfortunately, the strategy did not win him the game.

As you know, I myself am not a particularly good chess player, but I have always liked the game, and watching these two men play a good game rekindled my interest. Actually, more than that; it made me aspire to become – if at all possible – a better player. As for the idea of learning sign language – an odd-sounding idea – it comes, in large measure, from my having had my fill of hearing the sound of my voice and people reacting to that sound. You must be wondering what I'm talking about. If, after reading this epistle which promises to be longer than I originally intended, you end up with some sense of why I grew profoundly weary of hearing myself speak soon after I arrived in Roseville, I will have explained to you, I think, a great deal about myself. I know, of course, that sign language is not the answer to my problem, but I am interested in finding out more about it; in finding out, for example, what range of thoughts one can communicate through it, whether it permits communicating very abstract ideas. It surprises me that I never, previously, paid any attention to the existence of that language.

But back to yesterday, when, from a state of wanting to do nothing, I inched towards a state of wanting to do a couple of things. That it no longer seems so difficult for me to envisage returning to London is probably due to this welcome rush of life in me. Mind you, I am not quite ready to go. I would like to give Roseville more of a try. I'll stay here long enough to improve my chess skills (assuming that the two gentlemen are willing to play with me) and long enough to learn and practise sign language.

I am mightily relieved that the black mood into which I had sunk has begun lifting. Relieved for both of us. When I saw myself slipping into it, I was more upset for you than for me. The thought that you would be blaming yourself for my unhappiness bothered me greatly. That thought should have been enough to pull me out of my despondent state. I was unable, however, to stem the tide. I felt immensely tired, as if I had been running a marathon, or the way I imagine people feel at the end of one. They probably don't feel that way at all. They probably feel all invigorated, renewed, refreshed and ready for another long run.

The prospect of moving again does not seem quite so daunting any more. I tell myself that, after all, I am not so old. Only seventy-two years old, which counts as young in Sunny Homes.

Paris, you have gone out of your way for me. Well above and beyond the call of whatever duty you may think you have towards me; I personally consider you have none. Unfortunately for you, your reward was to see me become morose and virtually mute. True, I am taciturn by nature. But, I don't think that being morose is part of my nature. Moroseness is a different thing, though it is easy to mistake one for the other.

What must have been particularly galling to you was my unwillingness to discuss my reasons for feeling so low, which you must have interpreted as reflecting anger at you for suggesting I come here. You might have found it easier had I exploded and blamed you for Roseville's antiseptic, somewhat sterile environment (my need for busy streets, noise and even a bit of dirt harks back to my childhood); had I blamed you for the perpetually jovial air of its people – be it the staff in Sunny Homes, the staff at the library, the waiters and waitresses at the restaurants, or the receptionists at the doctor's office (they are all very, very nice but do they have to talk as if one was always in need of cheering up which, I suppose, I am, but don't care to be constantly reminded of?); or had I blamed you for being surrounded, in Sunny Homes, by people in a sad state of decrepitude.

Actually, none of this took me off guard. You had made a point of giving me a realistic account of what to expect. You had not hidden from me the downsides of the move. But shrugging off your cautionary words, I latched on to your suggestion the way one latches on to a lifebuoy. During my last arthritic bout in London – a particularly bad one – I was in quite a state. So, when you broached the possibility of my moving to Roseville and outlined the pluses and minuses, I embraced the idea, without giving the matter much thought, without even considering that, if I was prepared to live in a Sunny Homes type of facility, I might want to move into one in or around London. 'Why not Roseville,' I said to myself, 'as long as I have books, CDs and a quiet room in which to work?'

A couple of days after I arrived, it became clear to me, watching the streets with only cars zooming by, that adjusting wouldn't be so simple. Still, I tried to put on a brave face and focus on the positive side of my move, namely, your presence, as well as the fact that people are welcoming, and that my every need is taken care of. Then – and this was what triggered the downward slide – I was confronted with the fact that people here don't understand me. Yes, people in Roseville do not understand me. To be more accurate, they do not understand me when I first speak. I have to repeat what I am saying, painfully slowly, for them to understand. That is what really got to me. Were it not for the puzzled look on people's faces and the incomprehension in their eyes every time I opened my mouth, I honestly don't think that

I would have ended up feeling as weary as I did.

It wasn't the first time I encountered difficulties in being understood as a result of my accent, although in recent years, I've been spared that experience; London has become such a hotchpotch of people that accents there don't seem to matter any more. For sure, it was not the first time, but it was, as far as I am concerned, one time too many! At this stage in my life, I didn't want to be making the effort of having to translate my English into a more understandable English. I imagine you must be thinking: but wasn't this a bit of an overreaction? In an objective sense, it was. I myself was, to some extent, taken aback by its intensity, and yet I can account for it. That such a small thing should have had that sort of impact on me had a lot to do with my having experienced life – my entire life – as an exercise in juggling languages; with my being aware, almost always, of the particular language I happen to be speaking. One reaches a point when one no longer wants to be aware (or even worse, to be made aware) of the fact that one is speaking a language. One just wants to speak it, if you know what I mean.

Perhaps talking about a subject you raised with me long ago will help me explain myself better. The one time you asked me to describe to you the Alexandria of my childhood, I dodged the subject, intimating that I found it difficult to talk about that Alexandria without sinking into a sentimentality I am uncomfortable with, and, therefore, I preferred not to speak of it. I am generally uncomfortable with shared nostalgia. My experiences are mine; I can only treasure them if I think of them as unique. The few times – very few – I found myself talking about the Alexandria of my childhood, I had the impression that I was sullying cherished memories: trying to put childhood reminiscences into words, I would hear myself spout the same kind of nostalgic, romanticised account of that bygone Alexandria that countless others have given; and would end up feeling I was losing my Alexandria. Yes, I am possessive about my nostalgia. There are those who, less proprietorial, feel radically different about it, finding great satisfaction in the knowledge that their personal experience was shared by others. I am not one of them.

Not so long ago I turned down the opportunity to translate a collection of essays on Alexandria of the olden days. When approached by the editor I was tempted to accept; to see how it would feel like to be transported back into my childhood. However, no sooner had I started reading the essays than their exalted tone put me off. They all extolled the virtues of Alexandria, the magnificent Cosmopolitan. It didn't take me long to decide that I didn't want to be working, day in and day out, on writings that so glorify the Alexandria of days gone by. The writers – on the worthwhile mission of defending a certain cosmopolitanism – were, in my opinion, far too lavish in their praise of that Alexandria. Had they at all explored some of the difficulties associated with its much celebrated cosmopolitanism, I would have accepted the work. However, they simply ignored – totally ignored and not just glossed over – anything that might detract from their idealised portrayal.

A city of many languages: that is probably the most recurring theme of nostalgic evocations of Alexandria. And who can deny that there is virtue in speaking many languages? French, English, Arabic, Greek, Italian and, to a lesser extent, Russian, German, Hebrew, and Armenian. I have probably omitted some languages. Alexandrians of those days did not speak all of these languages. Many, however, spoke several of them. In my family, Greek, Arabic, Russian and

French were spoken. By different people at different times. I spoke Greek with my father and uncle as well as at school; Arabic with my father's helpers in the store, with the neighbours, and with the children I played with in the streets; Russian and French with my mother. English came later. I began learning the first rudiments of English only in the sixth grade. My mother hired a private tutor (a huge financial sacrifice, in our circumstances) for me to learn more than school taught me. The tutor had a memorable name: Ms Moneypenny. She tutored me almost gratis, so committed was she to my learning the language properly. Instead of the weekly session my parents could barely afford, Ms Moneypenny came, on her own initiative, three times a week for no extra charge. The readings she had me do were eclectic and included Enid Blyton, Wordsworth and Shakespeare.

When I say that I spoke different languages with different people, that is only one part of the story. In the course of a conversation, or even a sentence, one would often switch from one language to another. Under those circumstances, how well can one know a language: speak it, read it, and write it really well? And, even if, thanks to a determined effort, one manages to master a language, to what extent does it become part and parcel of oneself?

The very first time I met Ms Moneypenny, she asked me, 'Paris, in what language do you think?' I was twelve years old at the time. 'I'm not sure,' I answered, which was the truth. 'Think about it,' she instructed me. I thought and thought, yet thinking about it got me nowhere. So I came up with what I believed to be a sensible answer. 'Perhaps a bit in Greek, a bit in Arabic, a bit in Russian, even a bit in French,' I ventured to say in the best English I could muster. Not satisfied with this answer, Ms Moneypenny queried further, 'What does it depend on?' I was stumped. 'Does it depend on the person to whom you're talking, or on the subject matter of your conversation?' She was implacable, but I would eventually grow to be very fond of her. I took a deep breath and said, 'On what I'm thinking,' dreading the thought that she might ask me to elucidate, and give her some examples. 'Doesn't it depend on a bit of both?' she asked surprised. 'Oh, I don't know. I'm confused. It's confusing,' I burst out. 'It must be confusing,' she declared, and fortunately stopped interrogating me.

I may be an unusually impressionable sort, for her question never quite left me. I have asked myself several times, over the course of my life, 'In what language do I think?' and also 'In what language do I dream?' When I lived in France, I believe that I ended up thinking mostly, but by no means exclusively, in French; and when I lived in New York and London mostly in English. So paradoxically, Greek, Arabic and Russian, the first languages I spoke, have become just tools I work with, although, occasionally, I find myself thinking a thought in Greek, Arabic or Russian. I very rarely can remember in what language I dream.

In what language does one think? What is the language of one's dreams? What accent does one have? Even in cosmopolitan Alexandria, one's accent could be an issue – not a serious issue but, nevertheless, an issue. The children with whom I played in the streets, and for whom Arabic was a real first language, would occasionally make fun of my Khawaga accent. Other children – freshly arrived from Greece, or France, or Russia – would pass comments on the way I pronounced certain words in 'their' language. I'm not suggesting that I am representative of all Alexandrians of my generation. My linguistic background is rather more mixed than the average *background. However, to be fluent in more than one language without being in a position to identify fully with any one of them and claim it as one's own was not so uncommon amongst my fellow 'cosmopolitan' Alexandrians. My own lot was to end up having a universally foreign accent. Over the course of my life, I have so often heard people say to me, usually politely, 'I can't quite place your accent,' that I have taken to answer automatically, 'Neither can I,' which sounds rude but is the truth.*

At the age of eighteen and, thus, still in Alexandria, I convinced myself that I was meant to be a writer. A few compliments by a couple of teachers about the ease with which I seemed able to write in several languages had gone to my head. I decided to have a try at writing a piece of historical fiction – a novella. I had a specific idea which I won't bother you with. I researched the idea, took extensive notes in Arabic, French, English and Greek – the subject matter had been written about in all of these languages – got all geared up to write, till I confronted the question of which language to use. After much hesitation, I started writing it in French, then, considered switching to Arabic since I was living in Egypt, then, seriously, contemplated trying something really innovative and writing it in several languages. Then, I gave up writing it at all. I'm probably lacking any talent for writing. Still, I think that my inability to relate to one language and one language only – a language that would strike me as the natural vehicle for me to be expressing myself – did not help. It was after that failed attempt – my sole attempt at writing – that I began thinking of translation, for which, it turns out, I had a knack.

Have I managed to explain to you why I went into a state of hibernation, and why the idea of silent communication through sign language has some appeal to me? Or have I thoroughly confused you? I fear I may have done the latter for, to some extent, I myself am confused. I know enough about myself to know that I'm not the sort of person who wants 'to belong' – quite the contrary – and yet here I am claiming that I found it increasingly hard to socialise in the face of evidence that I don't belong! And I've always professed not to believe in dwelling on the past, and yet, am I not telling you, in a way, that I am the product of my past? I'll tell you something else that will probably confuse you: assuming I feel up to it at some point, would you care to accompany me to Alexandria? Not for too long a visit; still, long enough for me to try to catch a whiff of what may be left of my old Alexandria.

Tony

Other Worlds; Other Times
(Racy Subjects)

On the third anniversary of my aunt's death, I found myself thinking of her in conversation with her seamstress, Heba, with whom she rarely saw eye to eye but with whom she talked frequently. Their conversations usually concerned some member of Heba's family, and often involved an element of human drama heightened, in my eyes, by virtue of Heba's timid nature. My aunt was the very opposite of timid. She prided herself on being a decisive, 'no nonsense' kind of woman.

I was in my early teens at the time and couldn't understand why it was that my aunt could not put herself in Heba's shoes and view the world a bit more through Heba's eyes – at least for the duration of the conversations. Nor could I understand why Heba continued to solicit my aunt's views, even though she was aware of my aunt's inflexibility and would even complain about it to other members of the family.

In hindsight, I admire the fact that, while harbouring little hope of agreeing on any subject, they talked as much as they did.

They talked just to talk which, in the worlds in which I have lived since, people do much less of. That sort of talking can establish a personal relationship that has value beyond the actual exchange of ideas. It seems to me that, despite my aunt's peremptory tone, her conversations with Heba managed to achieve that.

For a few months, one of their ever-recurring conversations involved a most unusual occurrence. Heba's youngest sister, a young woman in her late teens, had been married for a couple of years. Sort of half-married really. Muslim marriages in Egypt involve two separate steps. First, there is the signing of the marriage contract which makes the man and the woman husband and wife on paper. Then, a party is thrown in celebration of the marriage. Right after the wedding party, the couple moves into their lodgings, and the marriage is consummated. The interval between the signing of the contract and the party can be days, weeks or months. And, when the two steps are kept separate, as is often the case, the expectation is that the husband on paper remains a husband on paper till after the wedding party. He can visit his wife at her parents' place, take her shopping, for a stroll, to the cinema or to a restaurant, but that is more or less it.

The young woman had been married on paper only. The actual wedding was a long way away. It was scheduled to take place once the apartment, which the couple was moving into, was fixed up and fully furnished.

One evening, the young woman complained of severe stomachache. Fearing appendicitis, her older brother took her to the nearest hospital. Two sisters went along. That very same evening, the girl gave birth to a full-term, healthy baby boy. When contacted, the dazed husband said, again and again, 'How can that be? How can that be?' He repeated it again in the hospital, while pacing up and down the hallway. Apparently, the young mother also said to the doctors, 'How can that be? How can that be?' The brother and the sisters were equally shocked. The doctors informed them that, notwithstanding the pregnancy, the mother had been a virgin prior to the delivery. They said that it must have been one of those freak accidents that can unfortunately happen when young people get too carried away before getting married. Really married that is! Meanwhile, the husband, still pacing up and down the hall, was bitterly bemoaning the fact that he had been deprived of his first night and honeymoon. As for the young woman's father, when told about the turn of events, he made it clear that the girl could not return to live at home under any circumstance. For any period of time. From the hospital, she would have to go straight to the couple's apartment, whatever its condition. The young woman heeded her father's words and, once released from hospital, together with the baby and her bitterly disappointed husband, she moved into an almost bare apartment. And began living her married life, under those inauspicious circumstances. Gradually, the husband resigned himself to his overnight transformation into a family man. It took a while before the young woman's father could get himself to pay a visit to the young couple. When he eventually did, he made a point of saying that it was only to see his grandson. It took an even longer while before he allowed the couple to visit him and her siblings at home. For months after that dramatic evening her family turned the story over in their minds and still couldn't fathom how it came to be.

When the subject came up, my aunt would often begin by

saying, 'There are two things I don't understand. Simple things. I don't understand how you all failed to notice the pregnancy; how even your married sisters didn't notice it. The other thing I don't understand is why you are all still so upset. The girl is married. She has moved into her apartment. The baby is healthy. The husband has a job and is providing for his family. Where is the problem?'

Heba would burst out, 'Believe me! I beg you to! Nobody had the slightest suspicion, although we had noticed that she was putting on weight, but the weight seemed to be evenly distributed. Besides, she always wears loose dresses. It is not as if we chose to ignore it. Why are we upset? Isn't it obvious why? Isn't it terrible to begin one's married life that way? It is neither good for her, nor for her husband, who still begrudges her what happened.'

Far from satisfying my aunt, that answer would have her exclaim, 'Are you siding with the husband? Turning him into a victim? How can he, of all people, complain?'

From that point onwards, the conversation would heat up.

'Of course I'm not siding with him. But this is how men are. They want their first night.'

'Well, he had it! Prematurely, but he did.'

'But he didn't have it!'

'Are you so sure of that?'

'The doctors said so! They were categorical about it. Are we not to believe them?'

'You never know. They might have said so just to pacify the family, knowing how you would react, had you been told otherwise. Maybe they thought that you would find that version of the story more acceptable.'

'You can't be serious! Surely, the doctors wouldn't do that!

They wouldn't make up such a story! Besides, it was clear from her husband's reaction that he hadn't had his first night.'

'What makes you think that he wasn't putting on a show?'

'Come now, are we then to doubt everybody? The doctors, the husband, my sister? Are we to doubt ourselves for not having noticed the pregnancy? Were we lying to ourselves? No, no, you are taking it too far! Why don't you believe the story as I am telling it?'

'Because I'm not a gullible sort. But let me go back to what really matters. The mother is healthy. The baby is healthy. The father is assuming his responsibilities. You should be happy. Treat them like a normal married couple, which they are. There is no point in making yourself sick over what cannot be undone.'

'You're right; they are married and, I admit, that, in the eyes of God, they were married when all this happened, but it is not so simple. Her married life has been marred.'

'You're complicating matters. Keep them simple.'

'Some things are right and proper; others are wrong. You, of all people, should understand that, since you yourself often speak of right and wrong. You're a woman of principles.'

'But I also know what is important and what is not. I do not waste my time on matters that have no practical consequences, and about which I can do nothing. If she had not been married, I would have understood your concern. But she is married and was married at the time the baby was born.'

'She was, but the expectation is for young people in their situation to wait. That is the way things are normally done.'

'To be frank, if anybody is to be blamed in that affair, the family is to be blamed.'

'You can't be serious! We are to be blamed?'

'You are, in a certain way. First, for not noticing the pregnancy, and then for giving her the freedom that resulted in the pregnancy. If it was such a big thing, you ought to have been more vigilant.'

'But we trusted them.'

'That is what blind trust gets you.'

'What should we have done? Policed them every minute they spent together? They were, after all, legally married.'

'Precisely! The idea of a two-step marriage is not a good one.'

'But is it good to hurry things the way they have? Not even a honeymoon has the poor thing had.'

'That can be fixed. They could have their honeymoon now. One of you could look after the child for a few days.'

'But she's breastfeeding.'

'Well, you can't have it all. If breastfeeding is so important, then let them delay the honeymoon until after she has finished breastfeeding.'

'By that stage, what sort of honeymoon would it be anyway?'

At this point in the exchange, my aunt would typically give up and sometimes even leave the room, making her growing irritation obvious.

* * *

The other conversation is self-explanatory. No background need be given other than to say that it concerned a different sister, who was also married. Fully married and apparently unhappy.

'Still the same issue?' my aunt would ask with raised eyebrows.

'Yes, still the same issue,' Heba would reply in a downcast tone.

'She's still fussing about that, after all these years?'

'Well, that's precisely the problem. After all these years. You'd think it would have gone away with time, but no, it hasn't; not in the least. Poor thing!'

'Well, try to put things in perspective. There are worse problems than that!'

'But it's not a life. She can't go on living like this. It's too much to expect.'

'Would she rather her husband divorced her? Would she rather he took another wife, or had a woman on the side?'

'Actually, yes! She says that she wouldn't mind him having someone else. She even suggested it to him.'

'Oh, I don't for a minute believe it! Mark my words, if ever another woman were to come into the picture, I'd immediately hear about how upset she was! So she's talked to him about this?'

'She has! Many, many times.'

'Did she really, or did she just hint at what is bothering her?'

'She was as clear as clear can be. But he won't listen.'

'Isn't he, all in all, a good husband? She should keep that in mind.'

'What do you mean, all in all a good husband? In that one most important aspect, he is terrible. A brute, really!'

'Don't exaggerate.'

'But he is! How else would you describe that sort of unreasonableness on his part?'

'To each his own!'

'But to want to do it three times a day! Three times! And

that is how it has been from the very first day of their marriage, and how it continues to be, after six years of marriage, when she has hosts of other things to do, including looking after her four children.'

'If I may say so, *that* is the problem. They've too many children.'

'It is God's will.'

'Well then, it's also God's will that she should have such a husband.'

'But God wants us to behave in accordance with reason – not like animals. My father knows about the problem but refuses to interfere. He says that it's a matter between husband and wife.'

'He's absolutely right.'

'But then what?'

Once my mother happened to be present at the end of this exchange so she suggested that husband and wife ought to discuss the matter with a doctor, to which my aunt retorted that people usually consult the doctor for the opposite problem, which made Heba raise her two hands, as though appealing to God, and she said with a smile, 'Let us hope he ends up with that problem.'

Meant for Each Other

He had arranged to be picked up at Heathrow. The cab driver was late. He was getting more and more tense. Should he forget about the cab and take the tube? The Tavistock Hotel, where he had booked himself a room, was close to Russell Square Station. The one and only time he had stayed at that hotel before was when he had booked thinking, mistakenly, that Stendhal had spent time there. It turned out to be a bland, functional, 1950s building without a whiff of Stendhal. The hotel's phone number happened to be in his address book so that was the number he had dialled on hearing of Nadia's accident.

Paris–London–Paris: a round trip he had done many, many times, over the course of a good thirty years. Always for the same reason: to see Nadia. Now Nadia was in hospital, hovering between life and death after an absurd car accident. He had heard about it the previous evening. His wife, Eva, had told him. A friend of a friend of hers had heard the news earlier that day. The accident had happened at night. And the friend had, of course, rushed to inform Eva who, to her credit, had related what she had been told matter-of-factly, without making any comment except for saying, 'I suppose you'll be flying to London.'

He was about to give up on the driver, when he saw a heavy-set man with a limp, waving a sign bearing his name.

'I'm sorry,' the driver – an *English* Englishman – said, without sounding overly apologetic. 'It's taken me forever to get here because of all the detours I had to take.'

'A lot of roadworks?'

'No, but Bush is in town, so you can imagine the problems. Police everywhere. They've closed a lot of streets. It'll take us a long while to get to your hotel. But what's to be done? What Bush wants, Blair gives him.'

As was often the case when he was in London, the sky was clear, belying the city's reputation for bad weather. Sunny and breezy; that was his image of London.

In the cab, the driver, who seemed to have an inexhaustible supply of opinions, talked about politics; about Iraq, the war, Blair, Bush, the French, the Russians, Bin Laden. 'And what about the veil issue in France?' the driver asked him. 'What do people there think about it? I'm not sure we're getting the full picture here. The papers tell you only so much.'

'They're divided,' he said in a tone that showed he had no desire to discuss the issue.

The driver took the hint, and was quiet.

Feeling he ought to explain why he was not keen on talking politics, he said, 'I'm here to see a friend who's in hospital; she was in a car accident.'

'You risk your life any time you're on the roads these days. It didn't use to be that way.' The driver relapsed into silence.

What would his life be like without Nadia? Around dawn that

morning – after a restless night, and with his wife still sleeping by his side – he had asked himself that question but then quickly brushed it aside, out of superstition (thought might make it happen) and also because he could not begin to imagine life without Nadia.

* * *

Cairo, 1954: the year they first met. They were both five years old, he was two months older than her. At this age two months matter a great deal. She was just a bit shorter than him. Pictures taken by his parents around the time of that first meeting show the two of them holding hands, she slightly bewildered, he ultra-confident. They were both only children. Their fathers were Egyptian. His mother was French, hers English.

He could never tell whether he actually remembered that first meeting, or whether he simply remembered what their mothers had recounted many times, over the years, since that meeting was to become part of the two families' lore.

Her mother was visiting his and had brought her along. He was in his room playing with his collection of small cars. At the sight of the little girl being ushered into his room, he grudgingly abandoned his cars, making no bones about showing his annoyance at having to stop his imaginary races. Then – and of this he must have a memory, since their mothers were no longer in the room (unless his imagination filled in the blank) – to provoke the little girl he was expected to play with, he suggested that they throw his cars – one by one – out of the window. And she, without hesitating, grabbed a car, rushed to the window and threw it. He had no choice but to do the same. One car after the next went cascading down the building from his parents' seventh-floor apartment, landing on Hag Ibrahim's newspaper stand. Not a single one of his much-cherished cars was spared. All of a sudden, his mother barged into the room, shrieking, 'Pierre, what on earth is happening? Hag Ibrahim is at the door with your cars in a paper bag. He's furious. He says that you've been throwing them out of the window. Apparently, you've been at it for the last ten minutes! What's the matter? Are you out of your mind? You come with me at once and apologise to the poor man!' And Nadia's mother, now also in the room, told her daughter, 'There will be no more playing this afternoon. You come into the living-room.'

They became best friends after that episode. Until four years later, when Nadia's parents decided to leave the country, not a week went by without his spending some time with Nadia, even though he went to a boys' school (an English school; his father's choice) and she to an all-girls' school run by nuns. They exchanged books (mostly Tintins and children's detective stories), played marbles, cards, snakes and ladders, draughts and monopoly. They went rollerskating together and swimming too, at the club. They even enrolled in a tap-dancing class together. And they talked. They both liked to talk. That they each had other friends (he strictly boys, and she strictly girls) did not seem to pose a problem. Every single birthday party of his, he put her name first on his guest list. When the time came for him to blow out the candles, she would sit by his side. At her birthday parties, he was the first to arrive and the last to leave.

'Turn off the lights, turn off the lights!' people screamed in the streets as he and Nadia ran inside the apartment and ducked into one corner of her parents' living-room, playing at pretending to be afraid (they later confessed to one another that they were actually afraid). They had been standing on the balcony when the sirens started blowing and the people screaming. It was 1956, the days of the 'vile and cowardly' triple aggression when sand was piled up high in front of buildings and people painted their windows dark blue.

'I wish my mother wasn't English,' Nadia whispered in his ear.

He whispered back, 'I wish mine wasn't French.'

They burst out laughing. Then, he whispered in her ear, 'I wish I were Hag Ibrahim's son,' which made her look at him with what he felt was boundless admiration. Two seven-year-old children huddled in a little dark corner, half-excited, half-afraid. When the air-raid warning was over they were almost disappointed.

Curiously, he could not remember his feelings when he heard that she would be leaving to live in England, though he remembered, very clearly, the goodbye party his parents had organised for her parents. Except for him and Nadia, there were only adults at the party, much of which he and she spent in his room, looking at his stamp collection. She too collected stamps but, of the two of them, he was the more serious collector.

They talked little that night. That was unprecedented. When it was time for them to say goodbye, and they were standing by the door, next to their parents, he did not know quite what to do – whether to hug her or shake her hand. His mother prodded him, saying to him, 'Come on, Pierre, give Nadia a kiss. You won't get to see each other for some time.'

The mothers hugged and kissed many times. The fathers slapped each other on the back. He gave Nadia a quick kiss and immediately proceeded to clown around, bowing and chanting 'Goodbye Madam, Goodbye Sir,' both in French and in English.

'You'll become pen pals,' her mother said.

They were ten years old; they did not become pen pals. At Christmas time, when their parents sent each other greetings cards, they usually wrote one another some insignificant line, at the bottom of the card, such as, 'I hope you're happy at school'; 'I'm learning to play squash. I'll teach you how to play when you return for a visit'; 'I'll show you London, if you come here.' But that was all.

She looked very young for her age – at least in his eyes – when he saw her again in Agami, a beach ten miles away from Alexandria with a few villas scattered here and there and which, twenty-five years later, would become a jungle of buildings. He was used to more mature-looking thirteen-year-old girls. She had come to Egypt to see her grandparents who had taken her to Agami, where he and his parents happened to be spending the summer. They became good friends – not best friends but good friends, with him being a little protective of her. He introduced her to his group – boys and girls buzzing with innocent flirtation. He told her, under the seal of utmost secrecy, that he had his heart set on Nevine – the belle of the group who was, very definitely, a very mature thirteen-year-old girl and wore a black bikini his parents found inappropriate. Upon hearing of his infatuation, Nadia said, 'She is very pretty,' without appearing to be envious or jealous.

One of the group's favourite games was called 'tell the truth'. They would all sit in a circle around a bottle which someone would spin. When the bottle stopped spinning, the person towards whom the top was pointing had to answer absolutely truthfully whatever question the rest of the group, by broad consensus, wished to ask. Whatever question! The questions were about love, though the word was hardly ever used. 'Do you like Nevine?' 'How much do you like Aziz?' 'Do you prefer Sami to Jimmie?' Those sorts of questions. Once, the top of the bottle had pointed in Nadia's direction, and the group decided to ask her: 'Do you like Egyptian boys or English boys better?' She blushed and protested, 'It's not a fair question,' which made Pierre feel sheepish for having gone along with the rest of the group.

Nadia went to Agami a couple of summers in a row, then she stopped going. Then it was 1967 and no one (or hardly anyone) went to Agami that summer, even though the terrible war was over in June. Pierre left secondary school that year and heard from his mother that Nadia had left too and was planning on taking a degree in art history. He would be studying economics, not so much because he wanted to but because his *thanawiya* marks met the prestigious faculty's tough entry requirements.

'Guess who is in Egypt?' his mother announced to him one morning in the summer of 1968. 'Nadia and her mother. They're here for the whole summer.'

This was to be the summer of his falling in love with her. The first time he would fall in love with her. He remembered the moment, that first time around, as if it had just happened. He was at the Ghezireh Sporting Club with a couple of friends, lounging around the swimming pool. Nadia, whom he had seen at his parents' place a couple of days earlier, was walking towards them when one of his friends remarked, 'Your English friend looks fabulous in miniskirts. They really suit her.' She did look wonderful with her jet-black hair contrasting starkly with her fair skin, her blue eyes and willowy build.

'I'm very fond of her,' he said gruffly to the friend. The message was clear: 'Don't touch her.' His friend understood.

It was probably the happiest summer of his life as she fell in love with him too. In fact, she told him that she had always been in love with him. When she returned to England, they wrote to each other constantly. She began spending every holiday in Egypt.

His parents were disconcerted by the turn of events. They approved of the relationship, but its intensity took them by surprise. They didn't quite know how to handle it. His mother told him that they were both awfully young to be getting so serious. While neither he nor Nadia talked of marriage, he thought of her as his forever.

They were both in their third year at university when her letters became less frequent. There was a casualness about her tone and an evasiveness that made him fear the worst: she was falling in love with someone else. He was right. In an awkwardly worded letter, she eventually admitted, in so many words, to having been briefly attracted to a student in one of her classes, but assured him that nothing had happened, that it had been an aberration and that it would never happen again. Never, never, never! She didn't know what had possessed her to even look at this young man. Pierre forgave her as best as he could.

When they saw each other, after the school year ended, loving her was no longer as easy as it had been. They quarrelled often. He began eyeing other girls. Just eyeing though. Was he doing it to spite her? Probably, as well as to protect himself, for what if she was to really stop loving him?

'From the most beautiful city in the world to the most beautiful girl in the world,' he wrote to her unimaginatively on an unimaginative card that showed lovers ambling along the Seine, the day he set foot in Paris to do a PhD in economics at Paris Dauphine. They were grown up now. Both were twenty-three years old. She had just accepted a job at the Tate.

At the beginning his move to Paris invigorated their relationship. They were free to spend weekends together and treat her studio apartment in London and his room in Paris as theirs jointly. 'Let's get married,' he said on a day he felt particularly in love with her, which made her laugh. 'But we already are in a way! Aren't we?'

Then what happened? He didn't remember the precise sequence of events. Paris was a heady thing for a young man who had lived all his life in Cairo. The cafés, the talk, the girls – in sum, all that Paris is known for. He didn't exactly cheat on her, but he was certainly taken by the whole ambience. She gradually lost the feeling of being central to his life. In those days, when she visited him in Paris, she wanted time alone with him, and yet he dragged her from party to party, from one students' meeting to the next.

News of her infidelity passed on by a not-so-well-meaning friend of theirs hit him in the stomach. Years and years after it had happened the mere thought of it still upset him. Confronted, she admitted the affair and fired back that, in any case, there was hardly any room for her in his life now. She said that he had in effect pushed her into the arms of that other man: she could talk with him, while they hardly talked any more. And when they did talk, they only talked about his life and his Paris.

'I never want to see you again,' he declared after they had exhausted themselves arguing. And, as if that was not enough, he added something he hadn't thought of saying – the words just came out – 'You'll never know happiness with another man.' She ignored his remark and pleaded with him not to disappear from her life altogether. She said, 'I need you. I need to know that you'll always be there for me, that I'll always be there for you. You can love whoever you want to love, whoever – I'm sure that part of you has been wanting to be free – but let's not sever all our ties. Let's keep something.'

He severed all their ties. Later, much later, though he understood what had made him say the awful things he had said – he had felt enormously betrayed – he was ashamed of himself for having said them.

Of course he fell in love again, after Nadia. He was young. It was the mid-seventies and Paris was full of attractive women. But never quite in the same way. After her, he would always keep a part of himself in reserve, however taken he was by a woman. Even with Eva.

Nadia he totally cut out of his life. As he had told her he would.

Three years after they had broken up, his mother told him that Nadia was about to get married to an Englishman. He sent her a card, saying, 'So you do prefer English boys to Egyptian boys, after all! I wish you much happiness. I do!' Did he though? To think of her still hurt him.

He got married a year or so after she did. To Eva, who was vibrant, smart, outgoing and pretty. Like him, she was an economist, and took her work very seriously. He liked that aspect of Eva's character. He also liked her calm and composed demeanour, her rational approach to life. But it was not a marriage of reason, nor a retaliatory marriage. He did fall in love with Eva. And he was very happy in his marriage at the beginning, then a bit less happy, but happy enough.

'Nadia's father died. It was very sudden,' his mother informed him over the phone. That would have been around ten years after Nadia had got married. They were both in their late thirties. They both had children. His mother suggested, 'We're going to London to attend the funeral. I think it would be a nice gesture for you to come along. You were very close after all, and you know how much she loved her father.'

He agreed to go to the funeral with his parents, who were by now also living in Paris. Why had he agreed to go? Out of curiosity? Because he and Eva were having a bit of a rough patch? In any event, that was how Nadia re-entered his life. And they were back, more or less, at square one. They fell in love again. His first extramarital affair. Her first too, so she told him. He chose to believe her. The affair lasted a little over two years. It caused them, caused Eva, caused Nadia's husband a lot of pain. On a quick trip to Cairo – a trip down memory lane, which neither Eva nor Nadia's husband knew anything about (he was supposed to be on a business trip in Syria and Nadia in Italy), they made up their minds that the affair must end, for neither one of them was prepared to break up their marriage. Despite all the love they said they felt for each other, they were not prepared to take a big gamble and dismantle the lives they had. Of course, the children – his and hers – were a big part of the decision, but it seemed to him, at the time, that they both feared botching it up again, as they had when they were younger.

Back in Paris, he turned over a new leaf, and threw himself more and more into his work. His marriage survived. He did his best to make it up to Eva, who had the heart and the sagacity not make him pay for the affair.

Years passed. He received the occasional Christmas or birthday card from Nadia but sent her none. Sometimes his mother would mention her. Once, he saw her with her husband at a big party in Paris attended by many ex-Cairenes, including some common friends of theirs. His heart sank slightly at the sight of her by her husband's side. Though she still looked charming, she had aged more than he would have expected, in the few years since their affair. She had lost weight and had become almost too thin. Her face was a bit drawn. Her cheekbones – one of her most attractive features – had become too pronounced. He introduced her to Eva: she introduced him to her husband, Peter. Everybody behaved with the utmost courtesy. The four of them were now solidly middle-aged, in their mid- to late forties.

Three to four years after that party his mother died. Accompanied by her mother, Nadia attended the funeral. It was a low point in his life. He was very attached to his mother. Her death left him feeling very alone. To have discovered, shortly before she died, that, for years and years, she had had an affair with a family friend – something he had never suspected – made him realise that he did not know her as well as he had thought he did, and that hurt. Nadia's presence at the funeral was timely. He was feeling the need to talk to her about the past, Egypt, and a whole range of things that suddenly seemed to matter, and which he felt incapable of explaining to Eva.

So he talked to Nadia. And talked and talked. And the talk led to the resumption of their affair. This time they managed to be discreet about it. Their feelings had lost their earlier turbulence.

Why they stopped being lovers he couldn't tell, but they did after a while, and yet they continued to talk and see each other in London or Paris, whenever they could. They became each other's best friends, as they had been when they were children and, as Nadia had pleaded for when he had said he no longer wanted to see her.

It was only after they stopped being lovers that Eva found out that he was seeing Nadia. Naturally Eva concluded that they were having an affair. He tried to reassure her, but how could he? He was not prepared to stop seeing Nadia. Besides, affair or not, theirs was a closeness no spouse would happily tolerate. In the end, Eva seemed to resign herself to Nadia's presence in his life. She continued to believe that they were having an affair, but she thought that he would eventually tire of it. More so even than when they had been lovers, he, though, could not conceive of a future in which Nadia would play no part.

* * *

After an extraordinarily long drive, the cab driver finally stopped in front of the Tavistock Hotel. Pierre had pins and needles in his legs and felt numb inside.

As he paid him the fare the driver said, 'I hope your friend'll be alright.'

Twenty minutes after he checked in, he went to the hospital.

Instead of a cab, he took the tube. It would be faster, he thought. And also thought that he should have gone straight to the hospital. Why didn't he think of it?

He arrived at the hospital too late.

* * *

'But you must go to the funeral,' Eva told him over the phone when he called her to say he was coming back home. 'I don't understand how you can consider not going. I just don't understand!'

How could he begin to explain to her that he could not face the funeral without being able to express the extent of his grief? That he couldn't face shaking Peter's hand, and saying he was sorry, when he felt that people ought to be telling him – him – they were sorry?

'No, you don't understand; you can't,' he told Eva childishly.

At first she was silent, then she said, 'I'm sorry, Pierre; I am.'

He sobbed his heart out after he had hung up. For all the losses he had experienced, all the sorrows, all the disappointments, all the defeats. The loss of Nadia had come to represent all his losses.

He forced himself to go to the funeral.

The next day, instead of returning to Paris, he flew to Cairo. It seemed to him the natural thing to do.

The day after he arrived in Cairo, walking in his old neighbourhood, he met Hag Ibrahim's son, Ahmad, who was a garage mechanic in the neighbourhood. Ahmad was about his age. Immediately after they shook hands Ahmad proceeded to pay him condolences for his mother's death: it was astonishing how news travelled from Europe to Cairo. They were reminiscing about the past when Ahmad said, 'I wish my father was here to see you (Hag Ibrahim too had died). He was very fond of you and loved to tell the story of your cars raining on his stand. That's how he used to describe what happened. "A downpour of cars," he used to say. He always ended the story by saying "the boy lost his head when he met Miss Nadia. These two were meant for each other." If you don't mind my saying so, my father never understood why the two of you did not get married.'

Pierre smiled feebly and said what any good Egyptian would answer in the circumstances, 'God's hand; it was God's hand.' He could not make himself tell Ahmad that Miss Nadia was no more.

Penance

'Far too pretty to be a housemaid,' people often commented when Basma was a young girl working as general help in Cairene households. And after talking to her most would quickly conclude that she was also far too clever. But she had an impetuous side: at sixteen, without telling anybody, she married a very poor but singularly handsome *mukwagi*, had two children (a boy, then a girl) in rapid succession, left the husband and the children when the children were still toddlers, found herself a cleaning job in an office (she could barely read and write) and promptly remarried.

This time her husband was a middle-class, government employee with a dependable salary and parents of some means. Basma's second marriage was thus a huge leap forward – a leap from poverty to a life of relative comfort, with meat on the table every day, holidays in Alexandria, a small family car, the service of a maid as well as that of a seamstress. In everybody's eyes Basma had made it. The pretty, bubbly girl with the upturned nose, winning smile, expressive eyes, delicate ankles and slim waist quickly turned into a plump, respectable-looking housewife. The face was still pretty and the smile still charming, although, curiously, she now smiled less often. In between smiles her face often acquired an ironic expression, as though she was about to say 'life is not quite what it appears to be,' or something along those lines. But the expression never lasted long.

By her second husband, Basma had three children – all girls – of whom she was immensely proud. And she brought them up with the explicitly stated intention of trying to shield them from making the one big mistake she considered to have made in life, namely, marrying rashly at too young an age.

Not long before Basma abandoned husband and children, I had been to the pictures with her. Or rather, she, at the time looking after me periodically, had taken me to the pictures. Her baby girl was with her. I was around nine years old. On our way back home, at a busy intersection, a motorcyclist lost control and ran into us. The baby girl fell from Basma's arm and hit the pavement. Basma immediately threw herself on the ground, very close to the baby, almost on top of her, encircling her with her arms as protection from oncoming traffic. Next, I fell. I don't know what made me fall. None of us was seriously injured. The fright had been bigger than the few scratches and bruises we ended up with. Once passers-by started diverting traffic around us we rose to our feet. The first thing I noticed was a big tear in my dress, which upset me more that it should have, but it was my favourite dress. Basma pressed the baby against her heart and, seeing a bump on the baby's forehead, she burst into sobs and, with a trembling but sharp voice, she cursed the motorcyclist, many times over, till she almost lost her voice. She was still sobbing as we slowly resumed our walk back home – slowly because of her sobbing, and also because my ankle was hurting. After howling for what seemed like a long while, which, we were told, was a good sign, the baby settled down.

The image of Basma throwing herself on the ground to shield her baby from oncoming traffic stayed with me for many days. It flashed through my mind when I heard of her deserting her children. The act did not fit the image. It troubled me to hear people denigrate her. 'An unworthy mother' became the leitmotif in the neighbourhood, almost every time Basma's name cropped up in conversation. I thought of trying to defend her, in light of what I had seen, the day the motorcycle hit us. But, merely a child, I felt ill-equipped to plead her case. I sensed that my evidence was unlikely to persuade her denigrators of her worthiness.

Basma stayed in touch with us after she walked away from her first marriage, showing up, at unexpected times, to say hello, inquire about everybody's health, and fill us in about her present life. Of her two children by her first marriage she never spoke. We, in turn, never asked her how they were. We had been told by some of her relatives that she had severed all ties with them; that she never sought to see them after walking out of their lives and leaving them in their father's care.

At first we were surprised that she maintained contact with us because we thought that she would consider us part of a past she did not wish to be reminded of, and because her first husband worked in our neighbourhood. We presumed that she would want to avoid the slightest possibility of running into him, or into her children. We were wrong. That eventuality did not seem to deter her from dropping in to see us about every couple of years.

Twenty years or so went by before Basma broke her silence over the subject of her children by her first marriage. As usual, she showed up unexpectedly, after having been out of touch for longer than usual. She looked more matronly than on her last visit. She wore a headscarf, but she had not given up on make-up or jewellery. The girlish vivaciousness that had always made conversation with her flow effortlessly was still there. Age hadn't changed that.

'So how are the children?' I asked after some gossiping. By then, we were comfortably seated around the dining-room table, each with a cup of coffee in hand. I meant, of course, the three girls.

Basma put her cup down on the table, but said nothing, which took me aback and made me immediately think that something must be wrong with one of the girls. 'They are alright, aren't they?' I asked.

Again, Basma did not answer. She seemed lost in thought. 'Is anything the matter? They're alright, aren't they?' I repeated, fearing that I was blundering in pressing the subject, yet I could not simply drop it now.

Basma's vacant expression became intense. She gave me an almost angry look, and said, 'When people ask me how the children are, I know that they mean the three girls. How could I blame them for thinking only of the three girls, as they are the ones I always talk about? In truth though, when I am asked about my children, I think of all my children. The five of them. One reason I don't talk about the oldest two is that I know what people think. They assume that I've stopped thinking about them. The other reason is that I feel I don't have the right to claim them as mine, considering I left them.'

'It must be an awfully painful subject,' I said lamely.

Basma sighed but seemed keen on going on. The words came pouring out: 'There's no denying that I left them. I did. The prospect of living the rest of my life in poverty and bringing them up in poverty got to be too much. Their father was a kind man. And very handsome when he was young, as you might remember. But every day was a struggle. Would we, or would we not, have enough money for the most basic groceries? I was young. I wanted to look half-decent. I wanted my children to have half-decent clothes. He didn't seem to care and, even if he did care, there was little he could have done. He was not in a position to improve the conditions in which we lived. Did you know that he was illiterate? I only found out after we got married. I found out by chance. He used to hold newspapers in his hands, pretending he could read it, but it was a show. He would listen to the news on the radio, and then claim to have read this or that piece of news in the paper, when he had actually heard it on the radio. He was no fool, you know. In fact, he was clever but had dropped out of primary school.' She sighed again and stated with a surge of intensity, 'Tell me, how could he have got ahead, without knowing how to read and write? When it became clear to me that he didn't know how to, I suggested he take a class. Some schools were offering classes for people like him. But he wouldn't hear of it. I saw myself condemned to a life of poverty. I saw no way out of it but to flee. I thought of taking the children, although I doubt he would have let me take them for good. He was poor but proud. He would have claimed them as soon as they turned the age when a father can claim his children. So what was the point? Besides, I myself was in no position to give them a better life. Unlike him, I could read and write a bit but barely enough to find a decent job. It occurred to me, at the time, that I might remarry but then what? Even the best of step-parents tend to be hard on their stepchildren; they're either hard or indifferent.' At this point, her cathartic outburst seemed to come to an abrupt end.

The first thing that came to my mind, and which I foolishly blurted out, after Basma said all this was, 'You were so very young when you had them.'

She winced. 'Sure, I was very young,' she said back to her measured tone. 'Still, young as I was, I was a mother, and a mother is meant to stay with her children, no matter what. After I left, I heard it reported by not-too-charitable relatives that people called me 'an unworthy mother'. It's not as if I didn't love those children though. As soon as I started working – I was lucky, I quickly found a job in a flower shop – I put a little money aside, every month, and sent it to their father to help with the expenses. At the outset, he typically sent the money back, but, as the years went by, more and more often, he kept it. After I remarried, without telling my husband, I continued to send him money. I stashed away some of the household money for that purpose. I knew that he was struggling to keep things going. You know that he never remarried. I'm not sure why.' Basma paused before she added with what sounded like self-mockery in her voice, 'At least, I didn't have to worry about how a stepmother would treat the children. I was fortunate that way. I knew that the money I sent wouldn't end up in a stepmother's pockets. I don't mean to condemn all stepmothers. Some behave honourably but, for every good story one hears, one hears many bad ones.'

'It must've been very hard,' I said, as empathetically as I could.

'It was,' she replied without looking at me. Then she stated matter-of-factly, 'I would also send them clothes, all brand new. I never, never sent Soraya any of the clothes that the three younger girls discarded, once they got to be fussy teenagers. I couldn't get myself to send her any hand-me-downs, even though I was tempted to, sometimes. The three girls are spoilt and buy more clothes than they need.'

'Did you ever see or talk to Mahmud and Soraya again?' I asked, uncertain whether it was the right question to ask.

Basma hesitated before she said, 'I used to see them, every so often. From afar. I used to stand opposite their schools, at the end of the school day, to see them come out. It upset me very much when they missed a day at school. I was left wondering whether they were sick, or whether they were just skipping school. I was certain their father would not be putting any pressure on them to stick to school and to study. A couple of years ago, when I heard that the girl was getting engaged to a young man with no education whatsoever, no technical training and no permanent job, I just about went crazy. I spent many sleepless nights wondering what to do. I considered having someone arrange for us to meet. I wanted to tell her to think hard before taking the plunge. In the end, I did nothing.'

'Did you tell the three girls about their older siblings?'

'Of course not,' she said, clearly surprised at my question. 'What could I have said to them? I abandoned two of my children?'

I suggested another cup of coffee. We went to the kitchen. While I was making the coffee, Basma reminisced with a laugh, 'Remember how upset your father used to get (may his soul rest in peace), when he saw you do anything in the kitchen? He had it in his head that you were clumsy – if you don't mind my saying so – and that you could easily set yourself on fire, or cut yourself with a kitchen knife. I told him once, "But how do you expect her ever to learn to work in a kitchen? She'll need these skills when she gets married." And he retorted impatiently, "Marriage, marriage; that's not the only thing that ought to matter in a girl's life." You know something? He was absolutely right.'

Back in the dining room, Basma said, 'You must be wondering why I am telling you all this now? You're probably thinking that I'm trying to justify myself, make myself look better than I am! That is not the case. I know that the little bit of money and clothes I've been sending will never make up for the fact that I left them when they were very little. I know that.'

'You tried to help as best you could,' I said, but my words rang hollow.

'I ought to tell you something else though. Now that I have started talking about the children, I might as well fill you in.' Basma crossed her arms, stared into space and continued, 'I have wronged these two children. That I know! But I've paid back and am still paying back. People rarely see beyond the surface of a life and, on the surface, mine looks good. Much, much better than it promised to be when I was working as a maid. Think of my background! I was brought up in poverty by a kind-hearted but struggling aunt; I barely went to school; at sixteen I married a man who had nothing and had no prospects of ever having anything. The few years I spent with him we slept on a mattress, right on the floor, and put the few clothes we owned in a big box made of cardboard. That's all we had. Now, I have all I need. In fact, more than I need. My in-laws are generous and, to be fair, have been good to me right from the outset, never begrudging the fact that I bore them no grandson. The three girls are spoilt but are doing well at school – in part, thanks to the private tutors we can afford. In all likelihood, the three of them will end up with a university degree. They can be difficult, but that's my own doing. I indulged them too much. At bottom, they're good-hearted girls. My husband lets me organise my life as I see fit. So it looks like I won a big lottery. It looks like I actually benefited from committing a wrong.'

Basma paused, uncrossed her arms and tapped the table lightly with her fingers. For some reason, this little gesture of hers reminded me of the days when, well before her first marriage, she would use a pot as a drum and dance, in the kitchen, to the rhythm of her improvised tune. Because of the mood she was in, I didn't dare tell her that my thoughts were drifting to those distant days; nor did I tell her how I used to imagine her then as a very successful belly dancer. I said nothing of the sort and waited for her to unburden herself; it was obviously what she seemed to be in need of at that moment.

'My life has been hellish in a major way,' Basma stated without melodrama in her voice. And then proceeded to explain. 'I never told you about it before. I see no reason to hide it any more. Five years after I remarried, my husband had a total mental breakdown. He completely collapsed – went out of his mind. It turns out that it was not the first time. He apparently had had similar bouts before we got married, but I didn't know. To see him in that state was very frightening at the beginning. I had never seen or known of a person collapsing that way. I'll spare you the details. We kept him at home for days and days. The doctor came to see him every other day. Fortunately, his parents could afford these visits. Eventually, he got better and got back to work. I thought it was all over. We already had two girls. I desperately wanted him to be in good health. For their sake, if not for mine. For a couple of years, all seemed well. Then, when I least expected it, he collapsed again. This time, it lasted longer. He became violent. We had to keep him in his room for days on end, and keep the girls away from him. He couldn't be trusted. Curiously, I was never the object of his violence, although his parents were. I seemed to know how to handle him. For some reason, he no longer frightened me. Maybe that is why he was more manageable with me. His mother would throw up her hands and let me take over. I became his nurse. As the crises recurred, he virtually stopped going to work and eventually stopped for good. He gets a pension. As you know, his parents are comfortably off, so they've been giving us money. Money is not the problem. Sometimes, my husband is fine. When that's the case, you'd never guess how unbalanced he really is. However, my love for him is long since gone. You can't love a man in these circumstances. You can pity him, care for him, nurse him, but love him? Believe me, you can't! The girls have come to accept that their father is a sick man. Maybe I indulged them because of their father's sickness.' At this point, Basma stopped speaking for a few seconds. I expected her to burst out crying. She did not, and when she resumed speaking, she spoke calmly. 'The story then is that, for years and years, I have had a husband whom I treat like a sick son. When all this started, I was at my wit's end, yearning, night and day, for the happiness that had so suddenly evaporated. I turned to prayer. I prayed that the good times return, that my husband's spells stop. Then, one day,

I found myself thinking that God had meant to put me through that ordeal. That it was the price I was paying for abandoning my oldest two children. Gradually, I stopped praying for my husband to get better. I didn't stop praying though. Now I prayed for God to give me the strength to deal with my husband, the strength to accept my bitter disappointment, and the strength to forego any hope of healthy, normal love. I told myself that, if I managed to be strong and patient and endure the ordeal without becoming horrible to my husband, God might be good to the children I abandoned.'

With a slight smile, she said, 'Yes, I tried to enter into a pact with God. I told him "Make me suffer, but be good to the children. All of them. The five of them." After that, when my husband's good phases lasted for longer than usual, I would get nervous, wondering whether the oldest two would end up paying for his good health! So you see, for a while, I too became a bit crazy.'

'You hid all you were going through so remarkably well,' I told Basma.

'Looking back, would I do it differently? The thought of living in poverty is as abhorrent to me today as it was when I was eighteen. That hasn't changed. So, would I do it differently?'

Nothing I could think of saying seemed right. I thought of telling Basma I was not really surprised that the two children had always been on her mind. I thought of mentioning the day the motorcycle hit us. But before I could come up with a half-meaningful way to say these things, Basma carried on, 'This week, I heard that the girl is pregnant. It has been on my mind ever since. I suppose that this is what got me going today, when you asked me how the children were doing.'

'A thousand congratulations!' I burst out which was probably the only right thing I had managed to say throughout the conversation.

Basma answered, wistfully, 'Yours will be the only congratulations I hear for that. A mother who leaves her daughter does not deserve to be congratulated on such an occasion. Still, it feels good to be congratulated. I worry a lot about her. Will she repeat my experience? Only God knows what is in store for that unborn child.'

After that, we talked about other things. Basma was hoping to go on pilgrimage to Mecca. The only obstacle was the unresolved question of who would look after her husband, in her absence, should one of his bouts recur.

Hand on Heart

'By the way, an old family friend might drop by this morning,' Nelly's mother told her as she was getting ready to go to the dentist. 'You've probably met him. His wife is the painter whose exhibition I took you to last year. Tell him I had to go out. He can drop by later this evening, if he is free and up to it. He can't do too much these days because of a heart condition. He's rather down and restless. When he heard we'd be spending some time here he called immediately to announce his visit.'

'Who is he exactly?' Nelly asked.

'He was a close friend of your uncle's. In their bachelor days, they used to party hard together. He must be well into his mid-seventies.'

'And what am I supposed to do, if he wants to come in in your absence?' Nelly asked, sounding annoyed.

'Invite him in, of course. Entertain him. It's not as if you have much to do today.'

'I may have nothing to do, but I don't particularly want to make conversation with that gentleman: he seemed like a buffoon the couple of times I met him, once with you, and once with my aunt. I like his wife though. Why she married him is beyond me.'

'Well, consider making conversation with him a charitable act. Talk to him about your recent trip to the Red Sea, or about university life. He has intellectual pretensions. In any case, chat with him. Find something to say.' Noting Nelly's wry face, Nelly's mother added impatiently, 'Don't make more out of it than it is! I must hurry now.'

She ignored Nelly's exasperated look when she finally set off.

Like a fish out of water: this is how Nelly felt since they had moved in temporarily to her aunt's villa while their apartment was being repainted. She hated the quiet, green, clean surroundings of Maadi, a garden suburb of Cairo, and counted the days till she would be back home in noisy, dusty, crowded downtown Cairo. Trees, gardens and birds chirping in the morning were not her thing. She was used to hearing honking, loud voices, and backgammon pieces slapped hard on wooden boards in downtown cafés, at all hours of the day and late into the night. She found Maadi's silence oppressive. A visit from this gentleman might be a welcome distraction after all, although she would not have admitted this to her mother.

An old gentleman with a heart problem would probably want to drink something on arrival. It was already hot, yet the day had barely begun. Nelly went to check what was in the fridge. Not much other than some freshly squeezed lemonade. Fortuitously, there was also some lemon cake, which tasted rather good with a few drops of lemon squeezed on it. So lemonade and lemon cake it would be, if the gentleman showed up. She would need a tray though. The one in the living room, an ornate silver tray, was probably too good for use, but Nelly had no idea where her aunt kept her everyday trays. Just as she was about to look in the kitchen cupboards, the phone rang. But where was the phone? For a few seconds, she couldn't remember. When she did, she ran. It was probably her boyfriend calling her. Though they were quarrelling a lot these days, they were about to get engaged. They had had a huge row the previous evening. Their frequent rows were often brought on by jealousy and possessiveness – on both of their parts, but he was more direct about it. She was more underhand, often pretending to be upset about some other matter, while he saw no need to pretend. He wanted exclusivity, in the fullest possible sense of the term, and made that crystal clear. Aware of the nature of their quarrels and their frequency, Nelly's mother, who thought their engagement premature, would often say that she didn't know which of them was to blame: they were both equally difficult.

'Oh, hi!' Nelly said, trying to sound indifferent.

...

'I'm not doing anything in particular; I have just started to organise myself for the day,' she continued with the same indifferent tone. 'What about you?'

...

'I'm sorry you had difficulties sleeping. I'm not the one who started it.' Her tone was becoming more animated.

...

'Sure, let's not start again but, really, you were so unreasonable yesterday.'

...

'I'm not starting it again. I was just saying you were intemperate.'

...

'What have I been reading? What do you mean by asking me that question?'

...

'What makes me use such a word? It just happens to be the one that came to my mind!'

...

'I can't take a joke? So I'm a humourless sort?'

...

'Well, I don't see what's so funny. You were sort of putting me down.'

...

'Alright! Alright! Let's be calm then. What I'll do today is try to read a bit. That's all. And a family friend may be dropping by. I'm supposed to entertain him.'

...

'Yes, it's a he, not a she; an old friend of my uncle's.'

...

'Look, the man is in his eighties – well perhaps a bit younger, but not by much. What strange ideas get into your head.'

...

'Not invite him in? You can't be serious. And what do I tell my mother when she gets back? Tell me that.'

...

'Men are men, no matter their age? You want me to say this to my mother? You want her to ridicule me, ridicule you, ridicule us?'

...

'I'm not naive. But I'm not crazy either. It would be crazy for me not to invite this old gentleman in just because you happen to think that every man under the sun is potentially dangerous!'

...

'Oh, please drop it.'

...

'Frankly, I don't know what to say to you any more. You put me in an impossible situation.'

...

'Alright, we'll talk about it later, when we're both calmer.'

...

'Bye!'

Nelly slammed the phone down and threw herself on the nearest couch in a rage. He had not told her how he had spent the previous evening, after their quarrel. She had called him several times, but he hadn't answered. Where had he been? With whom? Doing what? And now he had the gall to provoke another scene! Was it to avoid her questions? To avoid being put on the spot about what he had done with his evening?

The rest of the morning dragged on. Nelly tried to read but jumped at the slightest noise. The house made strange noises she was not accustomed to. She was hoping her boyfriend would call her back. Not once did the phone ring. Her friends seemed to have forgotten her since she had come to this remote location. And the visit by the old gentleman did not materialise. The book Nelly was reading, a book on the Second World War she had randomly picked from her aunt's bookshelves, didn't make the time go any faster. It was far too serious.

When Nelly no longer expected it, the bell rang. It was almost lunchtime. The gentleman at the door was the same rotund, short, bald gentleman she had briefly met twice before, except that his complexion seemed to have gone sallow. He was huffing and puffing, and seemed really quite old.

'Well,' he said, 'it's great to see you look so grown up all of a sudden. I can hardly believe my eyes. I remember you as a toddler.'

'Come in, come in,' Nelly said, smiling coyly.

'And where's your mother? Your aunt is in Alexandria. That much, I know. But I expected to see your mother. It's pleasure to see you, though.'

'Mother had an unexpected toothache. She apologises, but she had to go to the dentist this morning; it was the only appointment available.'

'One must look after one's teeth. That's one of the few things I've learnt in life.' The elderly gentleman winked, then added, 'I'll most certainly come in. How could I say no to such an attractive young lady?' Then, he raised his hand and patted Nelly's cheek in a grandfatherly way.

He knew the house better than she did and went straight to the living-room couch, where he made himself comfortable. 'Well, young lady, tell me about yourself. We met a couple of years ago. You were with your aunt. I remember thinking then that you showed promise but you have surpassed my expectations. How statuesque! You look like your aunt. I see a bit of your father in you too, although I could not say what exactly. I knew him well. He was a fine man. So was your uncle, with whom I had a lot of fun in my youth. A lot.' The gentleman then seemed to study Nelly attentively. She was still standing. 'Let us forget about the past and talk about the present. Are you at university already?'

'Yes,' she said. 'Would you like something cold to drink? We have cold lemonade.'

'I'll want some in due course. But don't stand like a pillar! You make me edgy! Relax. Sit down and tell me about university life.'

Nelly sat in the armchair opposite the couch.

'Why are you sitting so far? I am hard of hearing; like all old folks. Come closer, dear,' the gentleman ordered Nelly. 'Come and sit on the couch. Then I can see you better, and I might be able to tell in what ways you remind me of your father, a very distinguished-looking gentleman. The comparison should flatter you.'

Nelly complied, sat on the couch, at the opposite end, and started talking about her university. The gentleman seemed interested, asked pertinent questions, mentioned books she had heard about so she could pretend to have read them. All in all, the conversation was smoother than she had anticipated. The gentleman had a good sense of humour.

Suddenly, he interrupted her. 'Come and sit closer to me, I'll have a good look at your face,' he ordered. So she moved closer and continued to talk in an increasingly animated way. He interrupted her again, saying this time, 'Now I know; you talk the way your father did. That's it.'

Nelly asked, 'And how is that?'

And the old gentleman explained, 'You are as intense,' and he patted her knee.

To Nelly's surprise, he left his hand on her knee. 'Well, he is bound to be a bit forgetful,' she told herself but was, all the same, uncomfortable. She tried to ignore his hand and resumed her account of university life. The gentleman seemed to be losing interest in her tales. He was no longer asking her questions or making comments. 'Time to renew my offer of refreshments,' Nelly thought. Just at that very moment, she noticed that he was staring at her neckline. And was rubbing her knee with his hand. And before she knew it, he threw his arm around her neck, and tried to draw her face close to his, which was turning red. It was all so ridiculous, Nelly thought. He was going to injure his neck if he lifted his head up, as strenuously as he did. She, of course, resisted him – with awkwardness though, saying 'But no, but no,' – and had to struggle to disengage herself from his arm. When she finally managed it she jumped up and hurried to the kitchen, where he followed her and tried to corner her against the fridge. This was getting ridiculous beyond anything imaginable. The man was half her size and four times her age. Trying not to hurt him, Nelly pushed him away again and instinctively ran up the stairs leading to the first floor. When she heard him slowly climb up the stairs, all the while begging her to come down, 'Just for a little kiss, just a little kiss,' she ran up the second flight of stairs, leading to the attic. At the end of the staircase, she stood, totally still, next to the attic, dreading to see mice, rats, bats, or some other such creature suddenly creep out. She avoided looking up: all she could hope for now was that the old gentleman would lack the energy to climb up the second flight of stairs!

She could hear creaking sounds. The gentleman climbing the stairs? Then, all was quiet in the house. Nelly could no longer hear his heavy step. Where was he? She climbed down the stairs with as light a step as she could. And she saw him, leaning against the wall at the end of the first flight of stairs, hand on heart. All the redness was gone from his face. He was very pale.

What to do? Nelly's own heart began racing. He looked up, saw her and said, 'Help me down the stairs. I can't breathe properly.'

Supporting him under the arm, she led him down the stairs, back to the living room and sat him on the couch. He closed his eyes. 'Should I be calling his wife?' Nelly asked herself. She didn't have her number, but she could call directory information. Instead, she decided to ask him, with a clear and loud voice, whether he would like his lemonade now. Mercifully, he heard her, opened his eyes and mumbled more than answered, 'Yes, it's time for refreshments.' She brought him a glass of lemonade and put it on the side table next to him. They both pretended that nothing unusual had taken place – neither the chase, nor the heart problem.

When he left fifteen minutes later, some colour was back in his cheeks.

'So, did our visitor come?' Nelly's mother asked Nelly later in the day.

'He did,' Nelly shrieked, 'and let me fill you in!' she added with vehemence. Then proceeded to give her mother a blow-by-blow account of the morning's events. 'A buffoon and a scoundrel,' Nelly declared, theatrically, by way of conclusion.

Shaking her head, the mother exclaimed, 'My! My! It can't have been very pleasant, but you managed to look after yourself. Mind you, it couldn't have been that difficult, given his age and condition.'

'Mother!' Nelly cried.

'Some men are men till the very end,' her mother said.

'Mother!' Nelly repeated loudly, sounding the way mothers do when they reprimand their children.

Just then, the phone rang. Nelly happened to be standing close to it. She grabbed it nervously, not having made up her mind what she would tell her boyfriend.

...

'Oh, you don't really need to apologise,' Nelly said, in an exceptionally subdued tone.

...

'No, no, you had a point. One never knows.'

...

'Yes, he did come. I'll tell you all about it later. Mother is expecting a phone call.'

...

'No, I'm not angry any more. I overreacted.'

...

'I do too. Very much. I'll call you in the evening,' Nelly whispered into the phone.

Pasha, Be Careful

He was at the height of his power and he knew it. In his fifties and with more money than he had ever imagined he would end up with. Even in his wildest dreams. Money he himself had made – mostly in urban development. True, he hadn't started from nothing. He came from a well-to-do family, prominent in Cairo's Syrian community. The many connections had served him well. His great grandfather and great-uncles had held high-ranking administrative positions under Mohamed Ali and had been given generous land grants for years of loyal and efficient service. A rich and well-connected family is, however, never a guarantee of success. Many of his school friends, also from well-to-do families, had ended up squandering their family's assets, living the lives of *bon vivant rentiers*. Even some of his brothers had chosen to live their lives that aimless way. He, the youngest of the lot and the one with the least education and worst temper, had decided early in life that he must become very rich. He had had a carefree and frivolous phase in his early twenties, seeking amusement and romance all over Europe. But that had been short-lived. Making money was to provide him with a far greater sense of satisfaction than all his youthful adventures.

'Good evening, Selim Pasha; may God preserve your health, Pasha.'

'Be careful, Pasha; they have redone the pavement and left it very uneven. Fools! I nearly broke my leg yesterday. Better watch where you walk.'

'The paper will be at your doorstep at six in the morning, Selim Pasha – well before you get to the office. I know you like to start the day with a look at the paper. These days, the news is all about the quarrel between the king and the Wafd, and the possibility of a war abroad – news to give one a big headache. Have a good night, Pasha.'

'The dates are very sweet, Pasha. Just the way you like them. Tomorrow, I'll send my son to your office with a couple of kilos. I'll send you the very best. I will choose them one by one, myself.'

'Pasha, it is getting cooler; you ought to be wearing something heavier at night.'

'Pasha, how are the children? Still abroad?'

'Pasha, did you enjoy the peanuts you bought on Friday?'

'Pasha', 'Pasha', 'Pasha'. He enjoyed the sound of the word tacked on to his name. He did not have the title officially, but he more than deserved to be called 'Pasha'. Didn't Cairo owe him much of its modern, urban look? Walking downtown Cairo at nine in the evening, after tearing himself away from his desk to meet his wife at the Semiramis, where some charity was holding a function (for orphans, he vaguely remembered), it felt good to be greeted, left and right, by storeowners, newspaper vendors, fruit vendors, shoeshine boys and doormen. Did they like him as much as they let on? Probably not, but he didn't care. It was clear that they respected him.

Some family members had taken to saying that luck had been on his side. 'You twits,' he wanted to retort when they made these inane statements. 'Luck had nothing to do with it. Business acumen and daring, that's what did it!' He usually ignored their remarks, though sometimes he would explode: 'You're clueless!' he'd nearly shout. 'You think that it's luck that got me to gamble on buying land in parts of Cairo that nobody had thought of as potential residential areas, and which are now highly prized neighbourhoods? And was it luck that got me to gamble on building big, modern ten to twelve-storey structures for which I hired architects whose modernism you scoffed at, and now anybody into building anything is imitating my buildings?' Confronted with his anger, the offending family members sought to placate him, saying something like: 'Don't take it the wrong way. I didn't mean to downplay your many accomplishments – not at all! But Selim, you must learn to relax a bit! You explode over the slightest thing. Think of your health.' Far from soothing him, such words would irritate him even more. He'd have to make an effort not to respond with another outburst, not to scream 'Only those who do nothing worth mentioning can afford the luxury of relaxing and thinking of their health.'

Family was important to him – very important – but individual family members often got on his nerves; they could be so maddening. That's why he had taken to speaking loudly and volubly in their presence. He wanted to pre-empt their talking. It was not that he loved hearing himself speak, but he much preferred hearing himself to hearing their gossipy chatter and gratuitous advice.

Funnily enough, his sister's constant chatter he didn't mind. She was so absolutely self-centred that it was laughable. She never volunteered any comments about his character, or his life: it was always her life and the trials and tribulations of being a diplomat's wife. A diplomat's wife! What a joke! Her husband was a little consul (little in all senses of the word) – the consul of Brazil in Alexandria. There was nothing Brazilian about the man. He was just another Syro-Lebanese turned into a useless consular agent – basically a glorified paper-stamper. Poor Warda had insisted on marrying the man, despite his obvious lack of any redeeming qualities. Soon after the marriage she had discovered how little glory there was in the life of a consul's wife and, for all intents and purposes, was now leading a separate life. Yet she found it necessary to pretend she was not, and seemed to feel obliged to continue complaining about her quasi non-existent life as a diplomat's wife. But she had a great sense of humour. That is what made him, and others like him, half-listen to her flood of words. Nothing she said could be taken seriously. 'Warda lies the way she breathes,' people declared as soon as she was out of sight. Lies or no lies, she was entertaining. A born actress, and so she got away with it. Yes, Warda he usually indulged. He let her hold the floor.

His eldest brother Zaki, Warda's opposite in temperament, he had always listened to attentively. Zaki had been that rare and fine breed: a cultured man without any pretensions, as well as thoughtful, measured and perceptive. He had not shared Zaki's perspective on life. Yet hearing Zaki speak about any number of subjects used to force him to consider matters in ways he would not otherwise have done; unsettling ways, since they undermined the significance he attached to money and power. Their mother had once said to him, 'Zaki has a humanising influence on you.' He had not liked at all the implication of her remark, even though he had been vaguely aware that Zaki had this effect on him. It was not just what Zaki said but who he was.

Now, both his mother and Zaki were gone. His mother had died shortly after Zaki. The truth was that he missed him much more than he missed her. He missed his wisdom and kind wit. It still hurt him to think of Zaki's death, almost fifteen years ago – a death that had taken the whole family by surprise, although it should not have. Zaki had suffered from bad health for many years. They should have been prepared for the worst, but they were not. They had got used to the fact that long-suffering Zaki was often unwell. They had ruled out the possibility that he might succumb to his ailments.

After Zaki's death Selim would often catch himself thinking, 'What would Zaki have had to say about that?' However, there was one question he avoided asking himself: what would Zaki have thought about his breaking off all ties with Zaki's youngest daughter, even banishing her from family gatherings over which he presided, after she had married, in defiance of his wishes, a useless, penniless, glib talker, twice her age – a so-called cultured man, who lacked any business sense and seemed to think that he could live off fresh air and conversation? The girl had eloped with that idiot at the tender age of eighteen. And she had had the gall to tell him, the last time he had seen her in his office, which was also the last time he had laid eyes on her, 'But how can you object to him? You used to praise his wit and describe him as one of the few men in Cairo with whom you enjoyed having a conversation. You introduced him to me. And now you tell me he is no good. Why? Because he has no money? Well, my father never thought that money was all-important. I suppose I am my father's daughter, at least in that respect.'

Oh, he could have killed the girl for saying these things, right to his face. She had said them calmly, though it had been obvious to him, from the colour in her cheeks, that she was boiling inside. A pretty girl, promising to become even prettier, yet foolishly choosing a skimpy life for love! What she believed to be love! But what does an eighteen-year-old know about love? Spendthrift, Zaki had left little money behind, though he had worked hard. So the girl was left without much in the way of a dowry. Now, he, Selim, would have given her a reasonable dowry had she chosen the right man; he would have. He owed it to Zaki, whose tireless efforts had once got him out of an ugly legal pickle. He would never forget how Zaki had once shelved his legal practice to extricate him from a legal mess he happened to be in. And had succeeded, never asking anything in return. The silly girl would have got a dowry. With her looks, with her father's reputation as one of Cairo's finest lawyers and with the family's name, she could have aimed reasonably high. Her marrying this good-for-nothing older man had really upset him when the marriage took place, and he still got upset whenever he thought about it. He suspected that Zaki would have disapproved of his intransigence, and would have wanted him to be more accepting of the girl's choice. Well, he was not about to go and ask for her forgiveness now. It was out of the question. He had heard recently that money was becoming a real problem for the couple. That should teach her a lesson. He had warned her and warned her and warned her. What else should he have done? Surely Zaki would understand that he had acted in absolute good faith, taking his role as her guardian very seriously. Damn it! Why was it that, just about every time he thought of Zaki, he thought of the girl too, and ended up feeling awful about it all? This silly marriage of hers had managed to come in between him and the memory of Zaki.

The girl had been correct to point out that she was her father's daughter in attaching more significance to love than to money. Nobody had ever understood Zaki's choice of a wife – a mysterious, impoverished foreigner with a certain charm but nothing else. The woman had an air of vulnerability that made one want to protect her from life's many vagaries, which was not a good enough reason though to marry her. But Zaki had.

He, on the other hand, had made a solid marriage. When the time came to marry, he had set his eyes on Leila, a wealthy girl, whose father ran large department stores in Egypt. He had had no problem winning her father's consent. The father had wanted to ensure that his daughter would be on an equal footing with him financially, so Leila had entered the marriage with a substantial personal fortune, her father's stipulation being that every bit of it should remain hers. She could do with it as she pleased, but was not to give it to her husband. That condition had not bothered him in the least. He had understood perfectly well the father's wish to safeguard his daughter's interests. He had no need for her money anyway. He had wanted a girl with money, not to lay his hands on the money, but because he felt he deserved a girl with money and would gain from the boost to his status. Possession of this small fortune had given his wife an independence of mind and action that he, curiously, had come to appreciate.

Although not a love match, their union had proved to be a successful one. That she was a sensual, good-looking, buxom woman (perhaps a bit too fleshy) had cemented the marriage. His own physique left a little to be desired. Short, with a tendency to redden whenever he got heated about anything, and without any of the angular features typically associated with masculine beauty, he could not have won hearts on account of his looks. His big, booming voice was an asset though and made up for his insignificant physique. He had cultivated this voice, and using it was like a drug: he had become addicted to the effect that this big, barking voice of his had on people, relishing how they seemed to cower whenever he opened his mouth. Three people had been spared his big-voice treatment: his mother, Zaki and Leila – well, not entirely spared, for they had witnessed him in action, but he had never directed his barking voice at any one of them.

* * *

'Lost in thought, Selim?' He looked up, frowned as he detested being caught unawares, and muttered, 'Work matters, work matters,' while thinking to himself 'What bad luck to bump into him; I'm already late, and he'll want to talk endlessly. It'll be difficult to shut him up without offending him, and, if I do, I'll hear about it from everybody in the family for days on end.' The man whom he had met so inopportunely was the husband of a distant relative of Leila's. It was common knowledge in town that the man had married the woman for the tiny bit of money she had. Yet everybody felt sorry for him; she was notoriously bad-tempered and made him pay dearly, with her perpetual complaints, dark moods and suspicious nature, for every piaster she let him have.

He quickly decided that his best strategy was to try to expedite the meeting with joviality; so, tapping the man on the shoulder, he said, loudly and cheerfully: 'Butrus, you look so well; life must be treating you well these days.'

'Oh, Selim, things aren't going as well as you think. Salwa is very worried about the future.'

'Worried about the future?'

'Yes, I don't need to tell you that we're facing hard times. The price of cotton hasn't recovered; so she's getting less and less money from the land. She's not happy, Selim. She's not happy at all, these days. What do you think about the present state of the economy – here and abroad?'

'To discuss economic matters with this idiot is beyond my present abilities, really beyond them,' he thought to himself. Yet he managed a smile and exclaimed, 'Only God knows, Butrus; only God.'

'This is no laughing matter,' the man replied, sounding cross and then, lowering his voice, 'And what do you make of this ever-mounting nationalism? Just yesterday I overheard someone say, at the café, that we, of Syrian origin, are not Egyptians, that we are intruders and cannot be trusted.'

'Butrus, why are you all doom and gloom this evening? Lighten up a bit!' By now, he was getting irritated, and his tone clearly reflected it. 'Look, I must be going, or else Leila will be very annoyed. I was supposed to meet her at the Semiramis at eight-thirty, and it's well past nine. Say hello to Salwa, and do tell her not to worry too much.'

'What's happening at the Semiramis? A special occasion?'

'There's a charity function, with a lottery and what not. Don't ask me what tonight's noble cause is, I'm not sure.'

'But who's going to want to give any money? Everybody's concerned about the future. Now's not the time to give to charities.'

'Well, I can only hope that some charitable souls will be attending the event. Leila's counting on it. She's on the board of the organisation sponsoring the event. Look after yourself. We'll talk some other time, when I'm in less of a rush.'

'Go, Selim; go or else, as you said, Leila'll be angry. Pass on my greetings to her.'

'I definitely will.'

Phew! Free at last. He should hurry as it was getting late and, while he did not fear Leila's anger (she did get angry sometimes), he did not like to upset her unnecessarily. He liked to think of himself as a considerate husband. In her own way, she was also considerate of him.

So now, even a nobody like Butrus was running around, spreading stories about Egypt being in the grip of nationalist fervour. He generally avoided discussing questions of nationalism and identity. He frowned upon the tendency amongst some of his Syro-Lebanese Egyptian friends, to discuss questions such as: are 'we' Egyptian, and if not, what are 'we'? Why is it that they feel threatened by 'us'? Why do 'they' say that 'we' must learn to integrate with Egyptian society? Are 'we' not part of it? There were those – a minority – who said that the criticisms were justified, that 'we' were far too admiring of everything European. When occasionally he had expressed his views, it was to say that people have basically sealed their fate, once they start thinking in terms of 'we' and 'they'. For him, it was a straightforward matter: he thought of himself as part of the country. His skills and enterprise had contributed to developing its wealth. His parents and grandparents and great grandparents had contributed too. The family had done well in the country. So thank you, Egypt! But the country had also got quite a lot in return. The so-called Syro-Lebanese should be grateful, but the country should also be grateful. And as for this empty talk about identity and nationalism, to hell with it! Leave it to those without any appreciation of what makes a country's economy tick. Those with any economic sense generally ignored all this claptrap. Granted, some prominent figures had latched on to nationalism to further their special economic interests, hoping for whatever protection they could get under its umbrella, but these were men unable to stand on their own two feet. They were men without any intrinsic merit. He was getting all heated up just thinking of them.

He looked at his watch, and hurried. A couple more minutes and he would be at the Semiramis. He should have had the chauffeur pick him up, but he had been in the mood for a walk. Unfortunately, bumping into Butrus had spoiled the walk for him.

There was undoubtedly truth in the charge that, over the years, 'they' – the so-called Syro-Lebanese – had become culturally more oriented towards Europe. Had he not himself consented to Leila's wish to send the girls to school in Switzerland? On the other hand, he had been absolutely firm about one thing: the boys would be educated, from start to finish, in Egypt, as they would be going to Cairo University. He wanted them to be as fluent in Arabic as they were in French. If they were going to do business in the country, they'd better know it inside out. Europe was alright for the girls but not for the boys. Wasn't this a clear indication of the significance he attached to the country? This growing infatuation with Europe was more of a woman's thing anyway. Clothes and culture were more on women's minds than men's.

* * *

'Selim, slow down, what's the hurry?' Emile Z., the head of a large timber company rumoured to be in trouble, had caught up with him. They were almost at the Semiramis. Seeing them coming, two doormen were already holding the door wide open. 'The evening promises to be such a bore,' Emile Z. whispered to him, 'why don't we go in for half an hour or so and then retreat home – yours or mine – for a game of backgammon?'

'We'll see how things develop,' he replied, walking into the Semiramis to the doormen's profuse greetings and bows.

'Leila must be very pleased,' was his first thought as he entered the huge and sumptuous banquet room in which the function was being held. The room was packed. For Leila, the evening would be a resounding success as long as they managed to raise some money. There, in one of the room's many nooks, she stood, in a shining red velvet dress he had never seen before, talking in an animated fashion to a man who seemed, from a distance, rather young. He could not tell, from that distance, whether he knew the man or not. His eyesight was no longer what it used to be.

There were two – no, actually three – things he minded about these big, formal occasions. First, there were far too many people, and he hated small talk. He was not good at it. He much preferred intimate gatherings. In fact, what he liked best were the small parties Leila threw at their place. He liked to be the host. It gave him a measure of control. This whirling around in a large room, glass in hand, to exchange a few words with this one then that one, was definitely not his cup of tea. Young men on the make tended to love these functions for the opportunity it gave them to talk to the rich and powerful. Fortunately, he was well past that stage and had never actually played the game that way, even when he was young. He had always preferred private talks, in more private settings. Probably because he was not good at glib chatter, which was the strong point of this worthless Antoine, the man who had absconded with his niece. That man was in his element wherever he could talk, no matter how large or small the crowd was. Was there any chance he might run into him tonight? He very much doubted it. The man did not have enough money to come to these functions. But in the unlikely event of the couple showing up, he would simply leave.

So, he resented having to engage in small talk with a large number of people. And buffet dinners got on his nerves, however good the food was. He liked to be waited on at a table. Dinner was the time of the day when he could finally relax. Lining up behind a table with a plate in his hand was the last thing he wanted to do at dinner time.

The third thing he disliked about these sorts of occasions is that he often had to pretend to be jealous and put on a show of possessiveness. An inveterate flirt, Leila seemed to think that the bigger the event, the more flirting was required of her. At bottom, he did not care and, in all fairness, could not hold it against her. How could he? She had behaved like a flirt, even during their engagement. How far she actually went with the men she flirted with was not something he liked to dwell on. Very early on in their marriage he had given the matter some thought, and had reached the conclusion that there was no reason for him, neither sentimental nor practical, to stand in her way, as long as she was discreet about whatever it was she was doing. If she wanted to flirt in public, in his absence, so be it. But, in his presence, it was another story. Then he had to pretend he cared and, at some point, interpose himself. One evening, when he had had to do exactly that, it had occurred to him that she would be, most probably, disappointed, were he to keep passively out of the way. She too kept an eye on him during these big parties. One would have thought that she would welcome him being occupied with some other woman, which would give her the licence to indulge in all the flirting she wanted. But no, that was not the case. Whenever she sensed an interest on his part in another woman, and she had a sixth sense for these things, she quickly made her presence felt. She did have a jealous streak. But was it possible that she too was only playing the part of the possessive wife, while feeling little underneath?

A year or so ago a cousin had told him, under pledge of utter secrecy, that Leila was having an affair. He knew that the cousin was envious of Leila's social success, yet doubted that she had made up the story. He had assured the cousin that he would be keeping an eye on Leila, and, the very next day, he had asked Leila's favourite jeweller to deliver an emerald ring home. On the note accompanying the box that contained the ring, he had just signed his name. He did not know what had prompted him to send the ring. He could not explain to himself the meaning of his gesture. He had acted on an impulse. 'Lovely ring,' Leila had said the evening the ring was delivered, and had worn it ever since.

'Selim, how good to see you! I must confess that I had my doubts about your coming. I know how you feel about these sorts of events. They're not your favourite form of entertainment, but you're forgiven.' It was Bella S. speaking in her usual girlish voice. She was the wife of a man he liked, a clever financier who deserved much, much better than her. She was pretty but made it far too obvious that she was aware of it – something that really turned him off. In his eyes, her beauty was also marred by the fact that she could not string two sentences together without giggling like a schoolgirl. He had been mulling over whether or not to barge in on Leila's private conversation when Bella appeared by his side. Then, almost immediately after Bella, it was Jean K., whose principal subject of conversation was cotton prices, no matter the occasion. Then Sami M., who had inherited his father's sugar business, and let it run to seed. And Shukri Z., an intellectual poser but actually quite knowledgeable about a variety of subjects. And Ismail F., rentier and amateur artist, whose paintings were, according to Leila, starting to sell, and whom she had persuaded to donate a painting to the charity for the benefit of which the party had been organised. The painting was one of the lottery's prizes. So, all in all, not an entirely uninteresting crowd. Still, he felt hemmed in, standing there surrounded by them. And what he had feared would happen happened even faster than he had anticipated. Someone started talking about politics.

'Give me patience, God; now, I'll have to endure hearing one platitude after another. They'll rehash the same old stories and the same old ideas, and I'll be expected to say something insightful. What a waste of my time!' He was starting to regret having come, but told himself he must not show it. He'd give these people a few minutes of his time and exit discreetly with Emile Z. to play a game of backgammon at home.

Ismail F. was the one who started the ball rolling, asking 'Does anybody know the real story behind the students' gathering in front of the offices of Rose-El-Yusuf a couple of days ago, their demanding the author of an article about the Wafd to retract his statements publicly? Any idea who was behind the group of students?'

'Take your pick,' Sami M. replied, with scorn in his voice. 'It could have been the Muslim brothers, or these new extremists who call themselves "Young Egypt", or even these crazy Marxists, who, everybody knows, are funded by outside forces.'

Bella giggled, 'Somebody told me that these "Young Egypt" extremists really mean what they preach.' She giggled again, 'Imagine, they refuse, absolutely refuse, to speak any foreign language. They won't enter stores that do not carry Arabic signs!' She giggled again. 'And they'll only buy from stores owned by Egyptians, and they go so far as to refuse to buy imported clothes. And they don't drink. The funny thing is that they're apparently pushing for women's education!' Final giggles? Not quite, as she went on, 'The nephew of a friend of mine studied in France, fell in love with everything French, including a French girl, but, since returning to Egypt, has decreed that everything here is wrong, and that it is all the foreigners' fault, and so he refuses to speak French, has stopped writing to the girl and has asked his parents to find him a suitable wife!' Bella's giggle turned into a rather shrill laugh, which took forever to die down.

'Give him a couple of years and he'll come back to his senses,' Jean K. asserted.

'I wouldn't bet on it. He might join the religious fanatics, and then there is no knowing when, if ever, he'll come back to his senses,' Sami M. said knowingly.

It was Shukri Z.'s turn. 'What concerns me is that many writers known for their secular, liberal views seem to be turning religious. It's not just the fanatics who are the problem.' Then he said under his breath, 'We're among friends, so I can speak my mind. Let me tell you that the real problem is the palace. Don't raise your eyebrows, Jean! Believe me, the palace is a big problem. If the king was not playing the religious card to emasculate the Wafd (sorry Bella), there'd be much less trouble. And the irony is that, in the end, the religious forces will turn against him. He won't be able to control them forever and, mark my words, when the police start muscling in on these men – really muscling in – the king will be in deep trouble.'

'Talking about the palace, the Azhar paper has not given up on the notion of an Egyptian caliph,' Sami M. chimed in.

'Selim, why so quiet?' Shukri Z. asked. 'What do you think of the present situation? Students' discontent? Anti-European sentiments? Strikes in the textile industry? People thought that the treaty with England, extending Egypt's independence, would calm spirits down. It doesn't seem to have had that effect. What do you make of all that?'

Shukri Z. had put him on the spot. He answered, 'I'm merely a businessman. To talk about politics is beyond me. Zaki, whom you knew well since you were in his class at school, was the one interested in politics. He could have enlightened us tonight.'

'God bless his soul,' Shukri Z. said. 'Yes, we all miss him. I loved discussing politics with him.'

'But really Selim, you must have some opinions!' Sami M. insisted.

All of a sudden, he remembered a conversation he had had a couple of weeks earlier. 'Alright. I was having coffee with Mirit G. two weeks ago. He's writing a book precisely on these questions. His position is that the country is past the question of independence, that nationalism and religiosity are side issues, that the real questions are economic. Mind you, the man himself is an economist. In short, he says that what ought to concern us is poverty and the unemployment of the hordes of students graduating every year with degrees that seem to mean less and less. He is very persuasive. I asked him whether he thought the answer is a faster pace of industrialisation. "Absolutely not," he said emphatically. He favours concentrating on the agricultural sector. I'm not sure about that solution. It seems to me that there should be some balanced growth of both sectors. But I do agree with him that nationalism and religion are almost red herrings today.'

'Oh, Selim, you are so down-to-earth!' Bella almost shrieked.

'Well, I'm getting hungry,' he said, more pleased with his little speech than he cared to admit to himself. 'I'll see what these ladies managed to organise food-wise.' He left the group probably too brusquely, but then he had had enough. He wanted to say nothing more, hear nothing more.

Not a single dish of the dozens of dishes beautifully laid out on the buffet table tempted him. He pointed to a couple of appetisers, which the waiters behind the table heaped upon on his plate, then he started wandering round the room, plate in hand, looking for Leila. There she was, still in the nook. Still talking vivaciously to the same youngish man. What a fool he had been to tear himself away from his desk to try to be, more or less, on time for the event. Had he arrived much later, he would have been happier, and she would not have missed him. So what should he do? Interrupt her conversation? Simply leave and tell her, in the morning, that he had suddenly remembered an urgent matter he had to attend to, and had to rush back to the office?

For the second time in the evening he did not have to take a decision. Somebody took him by the arm, saying, 'Now, Selim, don't disappear on us; something tells me that you're tempted to do just that. I'm very tempted to leave too, but our wives would greatly disapprove, so let's make the best of it. Let's find a table where we can sit quietly, you and I. I'm thinking of branching into the property market and may come to you for advice in the next few weeks.' Things were starting to look up. Farid T., the man who had just taken him by the arm, was the sort of man for whom he had time. A man who was smart, open to suggestions, low-key and very successful in his line of business, textile production.

'By all means, do come and see me, any time,' he replied, perking up. 'Let's grab this table in the far corner.' He was already considering whether he should, one day, enter into some partnership with Farid T. If there was one man whose fortunes he might consider associating with his own, Farid T. would be that man. That he was Muslim was not an issue for him. In fact, in the current political climate, such an alliance might be a good idea. He ought to give the idea some serious thought.

The table to which he had pointed was at the very opposite end from where Leila was standing. Let her be this evening! After all, it was her evening.

Just as he and Farid T. were about to sit at the secluded table, a large group of men and women waved at them, pointing to empty seats at theirs. Both he and Farid T. smiled, nodded their heads in acknowledgement, yet proceeded to sit in their isolated corner.

It was then that he noticed a young, unescorted woman stepping into the room. Their table was close enough to the entrance doors for him to tell, despite his failing eyesight, that she was very attractive and was wearing no jewellery. At least, none that he could see from that distance. It was quite out of the ordinary for a woman not to be wearing jewellery at such a party. Her dress – a black, sheath-dress showing off her slender waist – was simple, flattering and elegant, but then anything would have looked elegant on that woman. Beautiful women who wore no jewellery always sparked his interest. He found the fact that they wore no jewellery seductive. It conjured up, in his mind, alluring images of nudity. Zaki too had been partial to unadorned women. 'Bedecked like Christmas trees,' his brother used to say derisively of many of the society beauties that happened to be the talk of town. The first time Zaki had introduced his wife to the family (they were married abroad), the only piece of jewellery she was wearing was small amethyst earrings. Lynx-eyed, their mother had immediately made a note of this, telling Zaki, while his sisters were entertaining his wife, 'Isn't she a bit too austere?' And Zaki had replied, smiling, 'That's one of the many things I love about her, Mother.' Leila, on the other hand, had always adorned herself like a Christmas tree – a fact Zaki had been gracious enough never to joke about. He himself had suggested to her, more than once, that she would look more attractive with less hanging around her arms and neck, but to no avail. She loved wearing jewellery. So, in the end, he had got used to her 'Christmas tree' look. But, every now and then, when he saw a beautiful woman walk in a room, free from the gold, the diamonds, the pearls, the rubies, and the turquoises typically adorning women in his circle, shameful but delicious fantasies would take hold of him.

He glanced at the young woman. He would love to meet her. He really would. Perhaps later. All of a sudden the evening acquired an unexpectedly pleasant complexion. First, the meeting with Farid T., whom he liked a lot and had not seen in a while, and now the prospect of getting to know this woman. He was about to ask Farid T. if he knew the woman, when two men surrounded her; and off she went with them, projecting a reserved yet, at the same time, a self-assured air. So he said nothing. Farid T. started talking business. He put the woman's fair skin, dark hair and slender body, out of his mind.

Talk of business and the young woman's image, which gradually

117

crept back into his mind, made him hungry. 'I'm famished,' he told Farid T., 'the appetisers weren't enough; let's get something more substantial.' At the buffet table, the dishes seemed more tempting than they had earlier. He joked with the waiters, who served him abundant portions, and told himself that he would have to remember to congratulate Leila on the choice of dishes. Not bad at all for a buffet dinner! As he and Farid T. were heading back to the table, with very full plates, he saw the woman again. And again, from some distance. The two men who had welcomed her in the room were still with her. A third one had joined the little group. The three men seemed to be talking to her, more so than with one another. She stood still, with a vague smile on her face. She seemed so self-contained. 'If I find out who she is, I'll send her flowers later this week.' It had been a long while since he had done that sort of thing. He used to send flowers to women who happened to strike his fancy for an evening.

'Farid,' he suddenly said, 'tell me, who is that charming woman, standing there with the three men? The one in the black dress. Probably the only woman here who's not wearing jewellery.'

'You mean the dark-haired, fair young woman?' Farid T. asked, sounding baffled.

'Yes, yes. That's the one.'

'But ... but ... Selim, is it possible that you don't recognise your niece, Zaki's daughter?'

The two men were silent for what seemed like an interminable time for both of them.

'I know that you had a falling out with her years ago, but don't you get to see her sometimes?' Farid T. said in a hesitant tone.

He felt so stupid, so stupid! For the first time in years – no, for the first time ever – he felt he wanted the earth to swallow him.

What a loss of face! His cheeks were burning. He could feel them. Shame on him! So that woman was his niece, Zaki's daughter? She would be in her late twenties now. He muttered, looking down, 'I haven't seen her in years.'

Farid T. looked at him, then looked at the young woman, after which he gently removed the plate from his hand, put it down on the buffet table, put his own plate down too, and said to him, 'She's a lovely and accomplished young lady; Zaki would be proud of her.' And, nudging him, walked with him towards her.

He let himself be guided. He could not say no. He did not know whether he wanted to say no.

When she saw them coming towards her, she quickly walked towards them, stopped right in front of him, and with a delightful smile, said: 'Good evening, Uncle Selim.' She gave him a light kiss on the cheek. It was as simple as that.

'If she is poor, then poverty suits her,' he had to admit to himself. She was even more lovely from close up than from afar. She was truly irresistible, totally unaffected. She seemed to have no idea how attractive she was. Desire dissolved into an immense, all-enveloping tenderness for this niece of his – Zaki's daughter. How foolish he had been to have kept her out of his life for all these years. 'Zaki, forgive me,' he prayed deep down inside. 'I am guilty, a thousand times guilty.' And she, after all these years, had greeted him as if everything had been alright all along. She had had the graciousness, tact and know-how to spare him any public embarrassment.

'What happened to your hair?' he asked a bit gruffly. 'It used to be much lighter.'

'I wish I knew, Uncle Selim. It just got darker and darker. I'm not used to how dark it has become.'

'And where's your husband?' Again his tone was a bit gruff.

'He's in Alexandria.'

'So, what are you doing here? Why has he left you behind?'

She laughed softly: 'Well, he is working, Uncle, and working very hard. He will be back at the end of the week. When he works very long days, I prefer being in Cairo than in Alexandria. He understands that.'

Without any transition, he said firmly: 'Come with me now. We must go and find your Aunt Leila, and then you must have dinner with us. We'll find a suitable table. And you, Farid, why don't you look for Nevine and join us for dinner? We would love that.'

He gave her his arm, which she took with much grace.

Arm in arm, they walked through the room in search of Leila who, he was certain, would be delighted to see the girl, having always taken the position that he had been far too uncompromising in this unfortunate affair but, since it was his family, it was not up to her to interfere. In reality, Leila rather liked the man his niece had eloped with. She found him entertaining and, until the falling out had occurred, used to invite him regularly to her parties, for his good conversation. Leila would be all in favour of a reconciliation.

As they were walking through the room, people were looking at them, or rather at her. He made a point of slowing down. She quickly adjusted her pace to his. 'This is happiness,' he found himself thinking, and he wished that moment could last forever.

Heat

'I must be out of my mind to be chasing after tomatoes at two in the afternoon in the middle of August in Cairo,' she kept telling herself, walking like a zombie under the scorching sun. She should have been napping – not on a pavement whose blistering heat she could feel through the soles of her sandals. But now that she was there, she wasn't going to turn back until she had found the right tomatoes – firm yet ripe, with the aroma of vines like those she had bought a couple of days earlier from an itinerant street vendor who had only tomatoes on his cart.

And why on earth had she decided to look for them in Kasr El Aini, one of Cairo's main arteries, a street that seems to suck up the heat as no other? She was too lethargic to change course, to think of where else, nearby, tomatoes might be found. She forged ahead, staying close to the buildings lining the streets, in the hope that the small patches of shade under their protruding balconies would give her some protection, if only for a few seconds. She suddenly remembered seeing a vegetable cart on a street corner not too far away. A couple of minutes at most and she would be there. It felt like an interminable journey. She threw a tired glance around her. Kasr El Aini was less busy than usual, yet the cars' honking was worse than usual. Incessant honking! Was this always the case on especially hot days?

She looked straight ahead and became vaguely aware of a commotion at the nearest bus stop. As she came closer she saw a woman with an infant in one arm, holding on to a man who was trying to free himself from her grip while motioning oncoming buses to stop. The woman held on to him firmly. Even before she reached the bus, she could hear the woman and the man shouting. By the time she reached the scene more than a dozen people, children as well as men and women of all ages, had assembled around them.

'I won't let go of him until he gives me money!' the woman shouted, addressing the small crowd.

'I told her a hundred times that I have no money; I only have enough for the bus fare!' the man yelled. 'Here, come and search me,' he offered, lifting his arms above his head as the woman continued to hold him by the front of his shirt. 'If she wants money, then she should let me catch the bus so that I can get to work on time. What sense does it make to keep me here when I should be going to work, if money is what she wants? You tell me!' the man asked the crowd, this time in a calmer voice.

'As usual, words, words and words! He knew very well I needed money for the child's prescription. Yet he left home without leaving a piaster. Not a piaster! He left while I was resting. Up to his usual tricks. He thought he could slip off on the quiet. Just like that! But I'm no fool. I was awake when he closed the door, so I jumped out of bed and followed him. I knew where he was going. Do you think that it's right and proper for a father to leave the house without leaving any money for his child's prescription?' Again, the question was aimed at the crowd.

Buses came and went but few people left the scene. By now the spectators were too involved in what was happening to be jumping on to a bus.

'Lady, perhaps you should let your husband go to work and you'll get your money later in the day,' a middle-aged man suggested. The man, holding a worn-out briefcase, looked like a government employee or a teacher.

'At last, some sensible words!' the husband exclaimed triumphantly.

The woman shrugged, turned her head towards the man who had offered the advice and shrilly said, 'Don't you understand that he won't give me the money? He won't give it tonight. He won't give it tomorrow either, nor the day after. He doesn't care about us. He doesn't care about his children. All he cares about are his cigarettes, his cups of coffee (dozens of them a day), sitting for hours on end at the café, and eating the meals I prepare. God only knows how I manage to put food on the table, twice a day, every day.' In the heat of her diatribe, the woman had let go of the man, who proceeded to tidy his shirt and tuck it properly into his trousers. Eyeing him with scorn and rage, the woman shouted for all to hear: 'If he were a man, a real man, he would be looking after his children and not after his shirt.'

Strangely enough, throughout the whole scene, the child had remained silent and looked in fact quite content, smiling at friendly faces in the crowd.

'Shut up and go home!' her husband yelled. 'If you're so concerned about the children, you wouldn't be running around town with this one in your arms, in this heat. Be sensible woman, at least once in your life.'

'If she needs the money, she needs the money,' a short but large and fierce-looking woman interjected in a dismissive tone, looking at the man straight in the face. Then, turning towards the wife, she said, 'God be with you; God be with you.' And as she said this, she waved her arms energetically, and her many gold bracelets jingled and glittered in the sun.

The husband hollered: 'You leave my wife alone. You stay out of this. You have no business interfering in our affairs. Stick to yours. I pity your husband.' He then walked menacingly towards the woman, at which point a young man jumped between them, putting his hand on the man's shoulder, soothingly. 'Don't get upset. She meant no harm. She was only trying to comfort your wife,' the young man said, sounding older than his years.

'I'm not afraid of him – not in the least,' the woman said defiantly, edging closer to the irate husband. Then she added, 'I know his sort all too well. Unfortunately I was married to one of them. God had mercy on me and freed me from that man. Now, I don't have to put up with any more nonsense. God be praised a thousand times for that.'

'No more such talk. You're adding fuel to the fire,' a man was heard shouting.

'What was I just saying? This woman's meddling in my affairs, turning my wife against me,' the husband said, treating the crowd as a jury.

The wife took a couple of steps in his direction. 'Enough posturing; get back to the real subject. Are you or are you not going to give me the money? Yes or no? I just want to hear a "yes" or a "no", and if it is a "yes", I want the money right now.'

The husband started unbuttoning his shirt in a seeming frenzy, shouting, 'Here, take my shirt, take it! And what else can I give you? You want my watch too?'

'Come now, don't disgrace yourself, it's not worth it.' Still sandwiched between the husband and the fierce-looking woman, the young man exhorted the husband to keep cool, while trying to restrain him.

A child in the crowd started to laugh, but quickly stopped as a man standing behind him slapped him twice on the head, telling him firmly, 'Stop misbehaving.'

'Let him take his shirt off!' screamed the wife. 'He enjoys putting on a show. That's what he's good at. He should've been in the movies.'

At these words the husband stopped unbuttoning his shirt, dashed towards his wife and was stopped in his tracks by three men, including the young man, who urged him, again and again, to keep calm. 'Think of your child,' one of the men pleaded, as the child started to whimper.

'What am I to do? What am I to do?' the husband kept repeating. 'She's sucking my blood!' he howled.

'And what am I to do? Steal?' the wife howled back.

The oldest and least well-dressed of the three men surrounding the husband reached into his own shirt pocket, got out a one-pound note and handed it to the wife, saying 'Here, take this and I beg you to go home.'

'Never!' screamed the husband. Then to his wife, 'Don't touch that money.'

'Don't worry,' she retorted, 'I'm not a beggar.' Then, to the man offering the one-pound note, she said 'You've a kind heart. God keep you healthy, but I can't take your money. You undoubtedly have children too. You must spend this money on your children – not on other people's.'

'Just take the money,' the man answered. 'God will make sure my children are well looked after. God is merciful to the generous.'

The husband, who would have none of this, said to the man, 'Don't embarrass me.' Then he snatched the one-pound note from the man's hand and stuffed it in the man's shirt pocket.

'It's only a very small thing,' said the man taking out the note again.

'No, no, no!' the husband replied angrily. 'May God be my witness. This money I will not touch, nor will anyone in my household touch it.'

As soon as her husband had finished saying this, the man's wife turned her back on the crowd. She walked away, the child on her hip, her slippers beating the pavement, saying out loud, 'This is no life. No life. I am fed up. Fed up. May God take pity on me and help me see the end of it all. Death is a hundred times, no a thousand times, better than my life with this man.' As she uttered these words, she looked formidably energetic – a woman destined to live to a very ripe old age.

The small crowd began to disperse.

It was time to start looking again for her fragrant tomatoes. She got out of the patch of shade from which she had observed the scene and heard the husband say out loud to the three men still with him, 'She thinks I can manufacture money! God be my witness, I spend nothing on myself. Almost nothing. The occasional cigarette, and I've cut down on those since the doctor told me to. And, yes, the occasional cup of coffee, but nothing else. This isn't a marriage. It's hard labour! Perhaps I ought to steal and go to jail. I'd be happier in jail than in my own home which, thanks to this woman, is a real madhouse. A crazy woman, as you had the benefit of seeing. But I'm the really crazy one – crazy for having married her, despite the many doubts I had. But you see, my mother kept urging me to marry her, praising her virtues. What virtues? And now my mother's no longer with us – God be with her – and I'm left alone to endure that woman. I was crazy to marry her and I'm crazy to still be living with her. I should've divorced her a long time ago.'

'It's the heat,' one of the men said by way of consolation. 'We're not ourselves when it gets so hot. She'll get back to her senses once she's at home. Don't dwell on what happened. She was worried about the child. She's obviously a well-intentioned, caring mother. Be forgiving. I'm sure that, at bottom, she's a good wife and a good mother. I can tell that her heart is pure.'

'It's true,' the husband conceded, 'she has a pure heart, but she can be so completely unreasonable.'

'Well, God in his wisdom created us all with some flaws.'

The men slapped each others' backs, wishing each other many good things. 'God be with you,' the three men told the husband as he finally jumped on a bus. 'God is great,' he replied as the bus departed.

The street was relatively quiet again. Time to trudge along in pursuit of the right tomatoes.

(Originally published in The Middle East in London, *Vol 1, No 4, July/ August 2004)*

They Took Everything

'But why won't you see them? I don't understand, Aunt Lizzie. It's so unlike you to be so intransigent,' the young man implored the old lady reclining on a chaise longue as he handed her a cup of tea.

'I don't feel like seeing them. That's all there is to it. I don't have to explain why to anybody,' the lady replied emphatically. 'Oh!' she exclaimed as soon as the cup was in her hand, 'the cup's too hot'; then she said, sounding profoundly irritated, 'would you please put it on the table.' The table was a piece of Art Deco furniture.

As always, the young man was struck by how both tasteful and distinctive Aunt Lizzie's apartment was. His Aunt Lizzie, really his great-aunt, had fearlessly mixed styles that most people would not normally have thought of mixing – Louis XVI, Queen Anne, Chinese, Islamic, African, Art Deco, rustic, as well as funky modern. Far from jarring, the ensemble made one want to linger in the apartment and get better acquainted with its owner, whom one imagined, from the mood created, as having an original but not overpowering personality. The furniture, the casually placed objects, were arranged in such a way as to make one's eyes wander from one piece to the next, without giving the impression that any single one was on display. More or less bare, the white walls brought the furniture and objects into relief, making the relatively small apartment look roomy. Large bay windows overlooked the Nile. For Cairo the apartment was relatively quiet.

The young man took the cup from the old lady's hands and put it on the Art Deco table, after making sure that the saucer was neither wet nor hot. This seemed to irritate his aunt, who said grumpily, 'Joe, don't worry about the table. It's there to be used, not looked at.' He ignored the remark and moved one of his favourite seats, an old Turkish stool with an intricate inlaid pattern, close to her chaise longue. With an unusually serious expression on his boyish face, he sat on the stool, rehearsing in his mind what he was about to tell her. A good-hearted sort, with a distaste for conflict, in particular family conflict, the young man was concerned about his Aunt Lizzie, whose health had been declining. Now was not the time for her to cut herself off from her brothers and sister.

That evening he had arrived at her place determined to make her reconsider her decision to see less of them. He was the only family member to whom she still talked on a regular basis, and whose visits she welcomed. Offers to visit from other family members she was now declining almost as a matter of course.

He was reasonably confident that he could mollify her, even though he expected it to be an uphill struggle. Her grievances against her brothers and sister were manifold. Her oldest brother, she accused of dishonesty, of having pocketed much more than his fair share of their parents' inheritance, and of having appropriated some of her own money. The youngest brother, his grandfather, she accused of being spineless, and her sister of being self-important. The whole lot she characterised as hypocritical. 'The modus operandi of family relationships seems to be hypocrisy,' she often told Joe now.

The curious thing was that his aunt had started expressing her bitterness about her family only late in life, a year or so after the death of her husband. Joe had initially thought that her husband's death had left her financially insecure, although money should have been of no concern to her: she was well-to-do. But the young man had observed some of his other elderly relatives become excessively concerned about money matters, for no good reason, from which he had deduced that it was one of those unfortunate things that can happen with age. It turned out that his Aunt Lizzie was aggrieved not only about money matters. She bore grudges against her father, long since dead, for having apparently thought little of her, from when she was a little girl to the day he died. Only her mother, also long since dead, escaped her criticism.

The young man put his hand on his Aunt Lizzie's hand. He had no desire whatsoever to hear from her, yet another time, the specifics of her allegations about her brothers' and sister's conduct. He feared that, by broaching the subject of the family, he would ignite his aunt's feelings and cause her to rehearse her grievances with abundant supporting evidence. He had no stomach for that and wanted to get very quickly to the heart of the matter, her obstinate refusal to have much to do with them.

His one and only purpose was to bring back a modicum of harmony in the family – enough for his Aunt Lizzie not to be so isolated at the end of her life.

What was in it for him? A good deal, but nothing tangible. Up until the sudden outpouring of her many resentments, his Aunt Lizzie had been seen by all in the family, including himself, as a model of generosity, tact and kindness; as someone who would never, never use her intelligence and wit to offend or denigrate others. He had grown up filled with admiration for the benevolent quality she exuded. He was not quite prepared to see her in a different light. It troubled him that she should be displaying that rancorous side. Her transformation from a big-hearted woman to a bitter one was corroding his childhood and teenage memories. And that bothered him. He could have concluded, as others in the family had, that she had lost her mind, but he saw no evidence of any diminution in her intellect and did not believe that to be the trouble.

Sitting on the stool, his hand over hers, he decided to appeal to her intelligence, as it must be obvious to her too that she had nothing to gain from her present attitude. And he would also appeal to her heart.

'Aunt Lizzie,' he said softly, 'what are you achieving by refusing to see them? You might look at things differently, if you started interacting with them again the way you used to. Your refusal to have much to do with them accomplishes nothing.'

The old lady shrugged and replied in a weary tone, 'Look Joe, you reach a stage in life when form matters little, even not at all. The very old become a bit like the very young in that regard. I have reached that stage. I no longer want to abide by empty conventions. I have earned that freedom. I want to say it as I see it.'

'I can understand that,' the young man said, 'but you've said your piece, and if you want to say more, go ahead and say it, but that's no reason not to see them. They know what you think, yet they still want to see you.'

'That's precisely the problem. Unlike them, I can't pretend that everything is fine. Once certain things are said, you can't reverse course. You can't interact, as if you'd never said them.'

Feeling encouraged by the way the conversation was going, as his aunt seemed at least willing to discuss the matter, the young man carried on. 'Look Aunt Lizzie, nothing is ever black and white. You yourself used to tell me that life is made of shades of grey. You're probably setting too high standards when you're judging them because you've always applied high standards to yourself. But Aunt Lizzie, one ...'

His aunt interrupted him brusquely, saying, with the sharpest tone he had ever heard her adopt with him. 'Please Joe, spare me this! Don't flatter me! Don't start telling me how good I am! If I were as good as you're about to suggest I am, I wouldn't be saying the things I have been saying about them, nor would I be declining their offers to visit. But I'm no longer interested in being, or in appearing, good. I hope you understand that.'

Undaunted, the young man persisted. 'But Aunt Lizzie, you don't mean to tell me that, all these years, you were playing at being kind and tactful and understanding. That would be untrue. You ...'

Again, his aunt interrupted him. 'Please, come to the point,' she said tersely.

'I'm not here to judge anybody. It could well be that my grandfather, Uncle Paul and Aunt Mary behaved badly. Still, they need you, and you need them. Put the past behind you. Please, Aunt Lizzie. Think of the bigger picture. They are family, after all.'

Laughing, his Aunt Lizzie said, 'So the young man is defending family values, and the old lady is spurning them. Well, well!'

'Someone has got to defend the family,' he joked, relieved at the change in her tone.

The change was short-lived: raising her voice she retorted, 'I don't care a wit about family.'

The young man hung his head. His initial optimism was starting to desert him. He decided to give it one more try. 'What is it that you would like, Aunt Lizzie? Please, tell me.'

'To be left alone.'

He pursued, 'What could they do to persuade you that they care, that they mean well?'

To the young man's amazement, his aunt replied, without any hesitation, as if she had given the matter much thought: 'To start with, they could give me some of our parents' possessions. They took everything, everything!' And with a dismissive shrug, she added scornfully, 'That will be the day, the day they agree to part with some of those heirlooms.'

'But Aunt Lizzie,' the young man burst out, 'what would you do with these things? You ...'

Cutting him off, his aunt replied, a noticeable tremor in her voice, 'Are you trying to tell me that, at my age, I have no need for these things since I have no children, whereas they do?'

The tremor made the young man aware that he had inadvertently touched on a subject that was very painful to her. 'Come on, Aunt Lizzie, you're being unfair. All I was going to say is that you have managed to create such a wonderful feeling in your apartment that I'm not sure any addition would enhance it. In fact, it might detract from it.'

She replied, not looking at him, 'I want my fair share of things. You can tell them exactly that, should they ever ask you what it is I want.'

He pinned his last hope on a matter that, he thought, might put her in a more benign mood. 'They were hoping to see you, next week, for your birthday – I heard them discuss it,' he said.

She did not answer.

He realised that more talk on the subject would get him nowhere. So he suggested a game of scrabble, a game at which she remained unbeatable. She immediately perked up.

That evening his Aunt Lizzie beat him by a huge margin. The young man left her, feeling doubly defeated. 'By the way, you can tell them not to worry; I don't want any more falseness in what's left of my life, but they can have and will get whatever I leave behind,' she said just before he kissed her goodbye. When he protested that money was not the motive behind their wanting to see more of her, she answered, 'Oh Joe, you're so naive.'

* * *

The morning of her birthday Aunt Lizzie's phone did not ring. Her brothers and her sister appeared to be respecting her wish to be left alone. Nieces, nephews and great-nephews, even her favourite Joe, did not call either. As usual her few surviving friends called in the late afternoon. She felt, she had to admit to herself, forgotten by all. But she quickly berated herself for waiting for the phone to ring; and for finding the silence of her apartment unusually oppressive just because it was her birthday.

Until the previous year, her brother, the one she now sometimes called a thief, had always sent her gladioli on her birthday. No matter where he happened to be, he would have an immense bouquet delivered to her door, first thing in the morning. Why always gladioli, she had never understood, or dared ask. Her favourite flowers were forget-me-nots.

The younger brother, Joe's grandfather, seemed to have a fixation on handbags. Every year she could count on his giving her a handbag. He would invariably tell her that he could not resist buying that particular one because he thought it was just her type of handbag. The handbags, all stylish, gradually came to occupy five shelves of her wardrobe. She had considered using a couple of them as decorative items in the apartment – some were by now vintage – but had never got round to it.

Her sister had been the unpredictable one. Her presents would be a true surprise – sometimes delightful, often disconcerting, like the imported bread-making machine that became a family joke since Aunt Lizzie hated gadgets, had never baked in her life and was unlikely ever to bake.

Just as she was thinking, not with total detachment, that this would be the first of her birthdays to go unacknowledged by her family, she heard a key in the door. The maid had arrived. That her presence would make the morning pass faster was Aunt Lizzie's immediate thought, although the idea of chit-chatting with the young woman – an enjoyable pastime on other days – had little appeal this morning. It would feel dishonest, on her part, to be pretending to take an interest in the woman's life – their main topic of conversation – when her heart was not in it.

Around eleven in the morning the bell rang, two quick rings – Joe's customary way of announcing himself. Aunt Lizzie, who had been lying on her chaise longue, closed her book and sat up. He had come after all! The maid let him in. Aunt Lizzie could hear him exchange the usual pleasantries with her. He was very good that way; he knew how to give a personal touch to any conversation.

The young man, still a boy in her eyes, marched into the room whistling and carrying several bulky bags which, before giving her a hug and a kiss, he proceeded to empty on the couch opposite her chaise longue, lining up several beautifully wrapped packages.

'What's all this?' his aunt asked, befuddled.

'You'll see,' he said, then added with exuberance, 'Happy birthday, Aunt Lizzie. Isn't it time for some cake?' And he gave her another kiss.

'Young man,' she replied cheerfully, 'did you think of bringing any? You won't find any cake in this household!'

It was true; she had no cake to offer Joe.

'Stupid me!' he exclaimed, tapping his forehead. 'You open your presents, and I'll run to the bakery. I'll be back in a flash with your favourites, apricot mille-feuilles and babas.'

Before she could say no, the young man was hurrying out of the room, urging her to have a look at the birthday presents he had put on the couch.

'But how come so many of them?' Aunt Lizzie asked. 'Have you won the lottery?'

'Not yet, but I plan to,' he answered and rushed out.

Except for one, which most probably contained a book, the packages were big. There were six of them in addition to the small one. Presents from her brothers and sister? Might that be it? But then why six packages? Mystified, Aunt Lizzie got up and started to unwrap the biggest package, which was heavy as well as big. It did not take long for her to guess what was in it. It was a table lamp, one of the many table lamps in her parents' house. The leg was made of copper and the shade of Venetian glass. The lamp was neither pretty nor ugly. She remembered it being used in one of the guest rooms that had also served as a sewing room.

With an angry expression, Aunt Lizzie attacked the next package. It was even heavier than the first. Halfway through unwrapping it, she recognised another of her parents' possessions, a round and nondescript crystal fruit bowl. By now her expression was positively sombre.

'Crumbs,' she muttered to herself. 'Crumbs,' she repeated, thinking, 'so that's how they're trying to placate me! They've the temerity to send me these things as presents! That beats all! They must think that I've become completely senile.'

Without bothering to unwrap the remaining presents, Aunt Lizzie returned to her chaise longue, mulling over what to tell Joe: it was best to say nothing. The sight of the packages on the couch – one opened, the other half-opened and the others untouched – would be enough to convey the message.

She was right. When he returned with a tray full of mille-feuilles and babas, his aunt's glum expression and the sight of the half-opened and unopened packages told him the whole story. Having his grandfather, great-uncle and great-aunt send Aunt Lizzie some mementoes from their parents' household had not repaired family relationships. It had failed miserably. Far from softening his aunt, it seemed to have angered her.

Normally easygoing, the young man felt a surge of anger well up – anger at his aunt for complicating matters and trampling on everybody's goodwill. For a few seconds, he stood right in the middle of the room with the tray still in his hands, telling himself to calm down. She was after all well into her eighties.

Her eyes shut, she pretended to be resting.

'Aunt Lizzie?' he whispered, suspecting that she was awake.

'Oh, you're back,' she replied and turned her head towards him. 'It was good of you to get the cakes,' she said, with what seemed to him like forced warmth.

He suddenly remembered the birthday cards they had entrusted him with. He decided that he would leave them on the hallway table, next to the front door. He would not give them to her now. Nor would he point out to her that, amongst the unopened packages, was his present, a collection of short stories by Patricia Highsmith, whose novels his Aunt Lizzie had described to him once, sort of jokingly, as appealing to her evil side.

'Would you care for some cake?' he asked her in a flat voice.

She could tell from his tone that he was upset and felt sorry for him. He had done his best to bring about a reconciliation, and she had let him down. She wished she had not. However, she could not make herself say that she was pleased with these absurd peace offerings. Joe would have to come to terms with the fact that the best of intentions can misfire.

They ate a baba and a mille-feuille each. In silence.

'Forgive me Joe, if I seem dejected today. I'm a bit tired,' she told him after they had finished eating. 'I didn't sleep well last night,' she explained apologetically. Then she praised the quality of the pastries.

His usual gentle disposition returned. She looked so feeble and frail, so vulnerable, that feelings of anger towards her seemed totally out of place. 'I guess you're too tired for a game of scrabble?' he asked.

'You're right, not today. Besides I wouldn't want to lose, just because I'm tired,' she said in an obvious attempt at lightening the atmosphere. Then she suggested, 'Let's listen to some music, something cheerful.'

He put on some light guitar music, then some easy jazz, then some accordion music. They didn't talk much that afternoon, but he felt good in her company. Being in her apartment often gave him the feeling of being in a cocoon. If she were to deny him the privilege of these visits, he would miss that feeling.

When the time came for him to leave, she told him more effusively than usual how much she had appreciated his presence. Then she said, 'I think it would be best for you to forget about these unresolvable family matters.'

On his way back home to his bachelor suite (his parents were still not reconciled to his living on his own), Joe wondered what to tell the family about the afternoon's turn of events.

After he had left, Aunt Lizzie quickly made up her mind that the packages on the couch must go. In the morning she would ask the maid to put them in storage. It was too late in the day for that now. She did, however, remove the smallest package from the lot and opened it. As she thought, it was Joe's present. She was touched.

* * *

Aunt Lizzie went to bed early on her birthday. During Joe's visit she had made an effort not to saddle him anew with her grievances against her brothers and her sister. As she lay in bed, she congratulated herself on having avoided the subject. She also wondered whether she would ever succeed in explaining to him, in a meaningful way, the origins of her feelings towards them. But how can one distil a lifetime of hurtful associations in a conversation? No amount of explaining can really do it. The few times she had tried, she had ended up feeling debased by it all, feeling mean and callous. The benefits of venting her ire had been minimal. So she was definitely pleased with herself for having kept her calm and having said nothing. And yet she was agitated. Sleep eluded her. It took longer than usual for her sleeping pill to work.

She woke up disturbed, in the middle of the night. She had dreamed of her mother. It had been a very long time since she had had such a dream. Her mother, looking sad, was sitting on a folding chair, at the beach in Alexandria. The image of her mother looking sad kept her awake for quite a while. She could not remember ever seeing her mother looking sad – angry, yes, but never glum the way she appeared in the dream.

It must have been dawn by the time she finally fell asleep again as the birds were chirping. This time she dreamed of her childhood. It was an adventure dream involving her brothers and her sister – a happy dream with a lot of running around and hiding behind trees. Yet the dream disturbed her.

When she finally got out of bed, she was out of sorts. Making tea she caught herself thinking that it did seem pointless to be making a point at such a late stage in life. So what if one of her brothers was not a model of moral rectitude? So what if the other was timorous and her sister rather a prima donna? The four of them shared a past, an indelible connection.

Aunt Lizzie checked the time. It was not long before the maid would arrive.

After her second cup of tea, which gave her almost as much pleasure as the first, she considered which one of her brothers or sister to call first, were she to call any. She leaned in favour of calling Joe's grandfather first, but wasn't clear in her mind on how she would deal with the sore issue of the presents, the mere thought of which immediately reignited her anger. She decided that only once the packages were out of her sight would she have enough peace of mind to consider seriously whether to call Joe's grandfather.

The maid found Aunt Lizzie waiting for her in the kitchen and received, right away, the instruction to put the objects and packages scattered on the living-room couch into the storage closet.

When the maid suggested, after much admiring the lamp and the bowl, that there might be a good spot for them in the apartment, Aunt Lizzie proceeded to leave the room, barely containing her exasperation at what felt like meddling in her affairs. But, just before reaching the door, she turned around to tell the maid, irritably, that she could take the whole lot home, if she wanted to.

'But ...' the maid began saying.

'No buts or ifs,' Aunt Lizzie interjected. 'Do you, or don't you want them, including the objects that are still wrapped?'

'I'll gladly have them,' the maid said hesitantly, adding, 'As long as you're absolutely certain that this is what you want. Are you sure that you don't want to open the packages?'

'I'm sure', Aunt Lizzie stated, and, the matter done with, was glad to hear the phone ring.

* * *

It was Joe's grandfather. He started the conversation by wishing her a belated happy birthday; then, not knowing what tone to adopt, he paused, evidently waiting to take his cue from her. She replied with a curt thank you, after which she was silent. Knowing that this would make him feel ill-at-ease, she felt a little sorry for him. He would have counted on her making conversation. Unlike his older brother, he was not so good at keeping a conversation going. As she was expecting, he too kept silent, so she made a move, and said, 'Joe stopped by yesterday. He's in good shape and seems happy.'

Much relieved that she had broached a neutral topic of conversation, her brother promptly agreed, 'Yes, he seems to be doing very well. He likes his job and seems to be very happy living on his own – an arrangement I didn't approve of initially. But it has made him more mature. So there must be some good in it!'

'I hadn't realised you were opposed to that arrangement,' she replied, in what sounded to him like an aggressive tone.

Seeing no point in arguing over such a subject, he backtracked slightly, 'Well, I'm not dead set against it, but ...'

Without giving him a chance to finish she changed the subject. 'Tell me,' she said, and this time there was no doubt about the nature of her tone – it was aggressive – 'why did you, Paul and Mary send me those odds and ends?'

This was a frontal attack. At the outset of any verbal

confrontation he was prone to stuttering. The stutter would go away as he gathered his thoughts. 'Well ... well ... oh, well, we thought ...'

Seething with indignation, she burst out, 'What's the meaning of sending me – for my birthday – things that belonged to Mother and Father?'

'Well ... well ... we thought that it, it would please you. Well ... that's ... that's what we were led to understand by Joe.'

'Oh, come on, George! Don't point the finger at Joe. Leave him out of this. He's not the culprit. He means well.'

'It was his suggestion,' her brother exclaimed. 'Joe told us that this was what you wanted.' By then, he had overcome his stutter.

'So you, Paul and Mary jumped at the opportunity to use my birthday to avoid settling outstanding accounts?'

'For heaven's sake, Lizzie, you've got us totally bewildered! We honestly thought it would give you some pleasure to receive those things. Call them birthday presents, call them family treasures, it doesn't matter. Does it?'

'It does,' she replied, with utmost earnestness.

'I guess I don't understand,' her brother said, cursing himself for having called her.

'Is that all you have to say?' she asked sarcastically.

'I don't know, Lizzie. Frankly, I don't. What more do you expect me to say? I could point out to you that, years ago, when Mother died, you showed no palpable interest in any of their belongings. You gave us the impression you wanted nothing to do with our discussions of how things should be divided. You seemed to look down on us for having these discussions. Now, we're hearing a different story.'

'And what about the money?' she asked.

'What about it?' he queried. 'Everything has suddenly become so complicated, Lizzie. It's beyond me.'

'Look,' she said more softly, 'if you really want uncomplicated dealings with me, then we must first resolve these issues. Have them all out on the table. All of these issues. With Paul and Mary present, of course.'

'As you think,' her brother said, shuddering at the thought of such a meeting.

'Thank you for your phone call,' she stated, clearly signalling that she wished to put an end to the conversation.

Formal goodbyes were exchanged. The conversation was aborted on that sour note.

* * *

For a moment Joe's grandfather thought of calling his brother and his sister, but decided he didn't have the energy to do so. His conversation with Lizzie had sapped it all. Putting up with Paul's verbosity and Mary's histrionics was, at the best of times, a challenge. He would call them later in the week. The three of them had really messed things up this time. They had followed Joe's advice too precipitously. It had seemed like a good idea though.

Joe's grandfather sighed, thinking of the time he had wasted, rummaging in his storage room, till he had finally unearthed the copper lamp. He experienced a tinge of guilt at the thought that he, as well as Paul and Mary, had chosen to send Lizzie 'seconds' so-to-speak; they were all items they had, more or less, discarded.

But wasn't the gesture supposed to be mostly symbolic? Surely Lizzie didn't really want any of their parents' possessions, which she had never liked? Her apartment was lovely as it was.

'Enough of these ruminations,' he told himself. It was best for him not to dwell on the subject, as it upset him and might cause him palpitations. His wife would tell him he'd been foolish to call in the first place. She would be right to say so. Yet he was not going to give her one more opportunity to tell him 'I could have told you so' – her favourite line. He would call Joe though. The boy was sensible and well-meaning, and had a way of putting a positive spin on things. Hearing his grandson's voice would cheer him up. He would call him immediately.

* * *

'Oh, hi Grandpa. How are things?'

'As well as they can be at my age. You'll know what I mean when you get to my age.'

'Did you hear from Aunt Lizzie?' the young man asked, somewhat hesitantly.

'I called her. She's not pleased. I suppose that's how things sometimes work out. You try hard but get knocked about in return,' he replied, trying to sound light-hearted about the whole affair.

'Grandpa, tell me, but only if you want to, why is it that she got nothing from your parents' house? I don't mean to pry, but I must say that I'm curious.'

'It's simple, Joe. When our mother died, your Aunt Lizzie expressed zero interest in what was in the house. More than that, she acted as if any such interest was beneath her. I remember her saying, at a family reunion, that she found the process of dividing family possessions akin to distributing spoils of war, that it was abhorrent to her. So what were we to say or do?'

'What about the money and the jewellery?' Joe asked, emboldened by his grandfather's seemingly candid answer.

'Again, she behaved as if she was above all this, and she intimated that acquiring more material possessions meant nothing to her, since she had no children and no need for money. Her husband had done quite well in his line of business.'

'That's curious! She told me the opposite, that having no children shouldn't have been held against her.'

'Well, she's free to change her mind, but why blame us?'

'And what happened between her and Uncle Paul?' By now, Joe felt free to ask virtually any question.

'Frankly, Joe, I don't know. All I can say is that she is, as you know, a very precise sort, and he's a man of many words – too many probably. There's often a discrepancy between what he seems to be promising and what he actually delivers. Now, what exactly transpired between the two of them, I couldn't tell you.'

'What about her relationship with her father? She does not have many good things to say about that. What was the problem?'

'Problem is too big a word. They had no affinities. It can happen between a parent and a child. He loved her, but he couldn't understand her, couldn't understand her inclinations, her left-wing politics, her never seeming motivated by material things, her generosity, her bookishness. He was much relieved when she got married to Samir, a practical man, who, my father hoped, would be the voice of reason in the marriage. She, on her part, saw our father as a ruthless businessman – which he was, in many ways, but there was more to him than that.' Joe's grandfather quipped, 'As you can see, family tensions didn't start with your generation. We had a flavour of them too. More than a flavour!'

Joe laughed and said, 'My own experience is limited, since I am an only child.' Then Joe asked, timidly, 'Did Aunt Lizzie want children?'

'Yes, she did,' his grandfather replied. 'She very much did, but it was not meant to be.'

They didn't speak of Aunt Lizzie after that. Their conversation turned to soccer.

* * *

Joe never again tried to play the part of the mediator between his aunt and her brothers and sister. She never completely cut her ties with them. They continued to call her, although more and more episodically. She was usually polite to them but icy. There were times though when she would tell them, with hardly any preamble, that she was simply not in the mood for conversation. Whenever she heard that one of them was unwell, she made a point of calling to inquire about their health, but always in a remote tone of voice. She evidently wanted to make it clear to them that concern was not the same as affection.

When she died from complications following a bad bout of bronchitis, just less than a year after Joe had delivered the notorious presents, the contents of a note she left came as a surprise to her brothers and sister. In the note she went out of her way to specify that she'd given the birthday presents to her maid so they shouldn't waste their time looking for them. They couldn't understand the fact that she thought it necessary to make mention of this.

But Joe understood, having discovered, several weeks after her birthday, that the presents had been objects relegated by his grandfather, granduncle and grandaunt to their storage rooms, which his Aunt Lizzie would have known. This discovery had given him a hint of where some of the problems between Aunt Lizzie and her brothers and sister may have resided. However, he kept his thoughts to himself when he heard family members comment that Aunt Lizzie had always been a touch odd.

Fracture

'Doctor,' his diminutive patient asked, 'would you care for more lemonade?' and, without waiting for an answer, she got out of her armchair with an agility that confirmed to the doctor – a man in his late thirties, more like an accomplished athlete than a doctor – that the time had come for him to put an end to the bi-weekly visits that had gone on for over six months. The fracture in his patient's hip had healed as well as could be expected. It was apparent that it would leave her with a slight limp but, from a medical perspective, his visits had become unnecessary.

'Perhaps, for a change you would rather have a small glass of vermouth?' his patient offered, eager to rush to the kitchen for more refreshments. Her desire to prolong his visit was written all over her face.

The doctor observed – in silence – that months of quasi-immobility had not altered her shape. 'Light as a feather,' he had observed when he first came to assess the severity of the injury to her hip; she had slipped on her bathroom's wet tiles. She had made it clear to him, in the course of that visit, that she did not wish to have surgery, even after he had explained to her that, without surgery, she would be at home for a good six months and in significant discomfort for the first few weeks; nor could he guarantee how well the fracture would heal. But it was up to her really. He hadn't tried to talk her into having surgery. Far from it. He was a surgeon who didn't hide from his patients his belief that avoiding surgery was generally a very good thing. It had pleased him to meet, in this small woman, a like-minded person with such a remarkable determination to let nature take its course, regardless of the pain and of how well her hip would heal.

To her anxious brothers waiting outside her bedroom, he had said, reassuringly, that her being so light would help speed the healing. 'But she's no longer young,' one brother had exclaimed, emphasising, 'She was born in 1889! She's fifty-one years old!' The other brother had mumbled, 'And what if she's left with a noticeable limp? I suppose marriage is no longer in the cards for her.'

In Cairo's Greek-Egyptian community – the woman was Greek, and so was the doctor – the story went around that she had squandered her youth and money on her two brothers, refusing this suitor, then that suitor, then that other suitor, all because she had been too consumed by her brothers' lives – first, helping them get established, then propping them up whenever they ran into difficulties. People said that she had never had a serious sentimental attachment – let alone an affair.

Did she look her age? To the young doctor, who had achieved fame in town not only for his skills but also for his looks, his liaisons and his beautiful wife, this fifty-one-year-old woman would have seemed old – definitely on his first visit. She had even seemed to exude what he would have described – if pressed to describe her – as that hard-to-define spinsterish quality that makes a woman undesirable in a man's eyes. Then gradually, over the course of the six months during which he visited her twice a week to make sure that her recovery was proceeding as it should, she seemed to lose that quality. He, at least, no longer saw it. What he saw instead was a woman falling in love with him. He could tell the signs for he was used to women succumbing to his charm. It was not a figment of his imagination. He was not a vain man. Self-assured, yes, but not vain. Good looks coupled with an air of confident virility, a quick wit and an ironic sense of humour from which he did not exempt himself, endeared him to all. It would have been surprising for a middle-aged woman, confined to her home, not to be stirred by his powerful presence, or touched by his generous solicitude. He took to charging her only minimal sums for his visits and only because she insisted on paying him.

His patient's infatuation with him had not been burdensome in any way. Reserved and unassuming in the extreme, she had behaved impeccably, never showing any signs of possessiveness. The doctor was confident that she would raise no objections whatsoever to his announcing to her that his regular visits had become superfluous, as she was in good enough shape to see him in his clinic – if this was needed. She would accept his decision with good grace. Nevertheless, he realised that the news would hurt her, which he would have liked to avoid.

There was no pressing reason for him to stop the visits. They did not inconvenience him. He stopped by when Cairo was still resting; neither he nor she liked taking naps. The visit would begin with his having either a cup of coffee or a cold drink and always some pudding her maid had prepared for him. Then, after examining her, he would chat with her for half an hour or so, in Greek, about all sorts of innocuous subjects, though once he found himself talking about politics. Not that she had a particular interest in the subject but she seemed so engrossed in anything he had to say that telling her about his political convictions had come naturally. He had gone so far as to divulge to her his association with a group of Communists that was trying to set up a Communist cell for Greeks in Egypt. 'Are you sure it is a safe thing to do?' she had asked alarmed and, in a tone suggesting she was prepared to shed her biases, had gone on to ask, 'Tell me, what makes a person become a Communist?' About politics, she knew very little, but was eager to listen and learn.

Over time, his visits had acquired a personal dimension. No medical reasons were needed for him to continue dropping in on his patient. The prospect of people gossiping about them – very unlikely in the circumstances – was no cause of concern to him. He never worried about what people said. Nevertheless, he did think it wise to end, or at least space out, his visits, while he was still feeling good about them. He didn't want them to turn into some constraining obligation. Besides, the longer he waited before telling her that he would no longer drop by as he had, the harder it would be for her.

'So, a little vermouth?' she repeated, surprised that he seemed lost in thought. This was not like him.

'You know I don't drink,' he answered, 'Only beer on occasion. Very rare occasions.'

'I might have a beer in the icebox,' she said. 'Or I could send for one.'

He smiled, 'Let me stick to my vice, cigarettes. I'll smoke a cigarette, then I must go. Come and sit down, though moving around is good for you.' And after this preamble, he continued, 'It looks to me like you're in pretty good shape. Almost back to where you were at before the fall. You could easily come to the clinic now, though you might need to walk with a cane at the beginning. So why don't we try it that way for a little while? For the next couple of months, you come and see me at the clinic. How about once every ten days or so?'

She sat down. Now it was her turn to seem deep in thought. 'So you think all is fine?' she asked, avoiding his glance. 'You think that I've recovered fully?' She still wasn't looking at him.

'What do you think?' he answered. 'You tell me. I trust your judgement.'

She looked at him and, nodding her head, she said, 'I think you're right. I'm fine, though it seems like I fell only yesterday. Time has flown since that first visit of yours.' Then, shaking her head, she said softly, 'And I who feared, at first, that the six months would never end! Things never quite happen the way you expect them to.' Then she changed the subject, insisting, 'But I must get you something to drink, some lemonade,' and she got up again, making an effort to make her getting up look effortless. When she walked towards the door, she tried to suppress her limp.

He let her get the lemonade, guessing that she wanted to compose herself.

After she returned, he talked about Metaxas and Mussolini and their different fascisms. He predicted that Italy was about to enter the war and speculated on how this would affect the British position in Egypt. He ended up saying much more than he had intended, divulging his idiosyncratic views on the subject and conveying the sense that he was taking her into his confidence.

Just before leaving, he decided, on the spur of the moment, to 'forget' his car gloves. It would give him an excuse to return later in the week and check on how she was doing.

She, however, noticed the gloves. 'Don't forget your gloves,' she said as he stood up. 'They're on the side table.'

At the door, he told her that she was his most courageous patient.

From behind the curtained window, she watched him walk towards his car, then climb into it. As he drove off she wondered whether he was going to stop at his mistress's place on his way to the clinic. The rumour in town was that he often did.

In fact, he was intending to call to see his mistress, but with reluctance. Indeed, if you had asked him he would have said that 'mistress' had become a misnomer for the woman he was seeing just about every day on his way to his clinic. A long-standing liaison ripe enough to turn into a friendship: this was how he had come to feel about that attachment, as he was not a man who liked to sever all his ties with the women he had once loved. The problem was that his mistress didn't see it that way, still wanting what was no longer on offer.

That late afternoon, he felt even less inclined than usual to pay his mistress a call. He dreaded her accusatory glances which she alternated with a sad gaze, though she sometimes managed to put on a show of extreme cheerfulness, unconvincingly extreme.

He drove slowly to his mistress's place, thinking about his patient. He would miss those visits; he would much rather still be visiting her than going to his mistress. He now recognised that it was not only out of concern for his patient's feelings that he had had qualms about telling her that his visits were, more or less, over. He himself had come to depend on this woman's warm welcome, her silent but palpable gratitude, and the seemingly unconditional admiration in which she held him. For the first time, he wondered whether she really had had as barren a sentimental life as people said she had. He tried to picture her when she was younger.

By now he had arrived in front of his mistress's apartment. He hesitated for a moment before he opened the car door. When he got out he seemed preoccupied. Looking out of the window, his mistress saw him walk towards her building. He looked up. She quickly stepped back, and went straight to the nearest mirror in the room to tidy her hair. Trying to put her mind at rest, she told herself, 'Well, he's bound to enjoy being here, for it's Tuesday, so he must have just finished visiting the old maid.'

Turbulence

Cairo–London in early March: I was counting on the flight being half-empty; it was packed. Not a single empty seat, though it was neither the beginning nor the end of the holiday season. Just the normal flow of people going to London. Quite a few businessmen as well as tourists, despite the war in Iraq and fundamentalism and al-Qaeda. During a tedious business dinner held on the evening of my departure, a government official had informed me, proudly, that tourism was at a record high. Eight million tourists had come to Egypt that year, the antiquities' inspector had declared, reflecting on 'how just four years ago, after 9/11, the hotels were empty; Luxor was empty; Sharm El Sheikh was empty. And now, you have to book, months ahead of time, to get a room.'

I was very tired the next morning; the dinner had lasted well past my bedtime, and I had barely slept after having the stupidest of arguments with Jack over the phone. I had woken him up. I knew I would, but I wanted to tell him I was missing him a lot that evening, and also about a conversation I'd had with a cab driver earlier. My missing him had something to do with that conversation. Jack's tepid reception of my call – understandable at that time of the night – had upset me though. And when he told me that he wouldn't be home for lunch or dinner next day – he was tied up at work – I got huffy. Without rhyme or reason, I suggested that, had he really wanted to, he could have easily taken a short break to join me in Cairo; I could have shown him many things about the city he still knew little of. As if this not-so-veiled complaint was not enough, I then proceeded to blame us both for letting our work get the better of our lives. He interjected in his most paternal tone – a tone I really dislike – 'Don't dramatize things. We're doing alright.' That killed my desire to tell him the cab driver's story.

After hanging up abruptly I spent a long time awake in bed, mad at Jack and regretting calling him, and feeling sheepish that fifteen years of a reasonably happy marriage had not taught me to refrain from uttering the nonsense I sometimes uttered, whenever we were not on the same wavelength. While I lay in bed, trying to reason myself out of – though, in effect, into – my negative state of mind, the cab driver's story kept flitting through my mind.

* * *

A call on his mobile had put the cab driver in a jubilant mood, judging by how effervescently he replied to the caller. Then he told me the news that, just a few minutes earlier, his wife had been taken to hospital to give birth to their fourth child. 'My sister,' he said, which was a somewhat unusual form of address, in the circumstances, 'My wife is my cousin, but more than that, she is my soul. We've been married for fourteen years. I'd do anything for her. And I'm certain that she would do anything for me. Her happiness is my happiness. She understands me better than I understand myself, and she knows how to take me. She's my life. We don't have much, but we are happy. Our three girls are fine girls. In good health, thank God. My wife would like to have a boy now, but I tell her, "Why a boy?" In this day and age, a girl is just as good. Today, a girl can be a doctor, an engineer, even a minister. My sister, I would be as happy with a girl as with a boy. But my wife wants a boy. All I want is her good health. I cannot conceive of life without her.'

He wasn't driving me very far, only from the Marriott to the Hilton. Since it was Friday noontime – prayer time – the streets were almost empty. By the time the driver had told me all this, we were nearing the Hilton. I had already set aside, in the outer pocket of my handbag, a ten-pound note for the fare – reasonably generous for the distance, but certainly not enough for the very special occasion I had just heard about. As I opened the cab door, 'Should I tip him more generously or not?' flashed through my mind, but so did the question, 'Is this a made-up, well-rehearsed story he tells women customers he suspects of being feminists?' In the end, I only gave him the ten pounds, partly because I didn't know how much more to give.

True or not, it was a nice story. So, no sooner had I gotten out of the taxi than I was angry with myself for not having given the man a more substantial tip. My friends waiting at the Hilton decided that his account had an authentic ring. 'The man should be interviewed on TV as the exemplary husband,' a recently divorced friend exclaimed. 'He's got the right angle on things.'

* * *

It's curious how much one can make out of a seemingly insignificant occurrence. On the eve of my return to London, awake in my hotel room, thinking about the driver's marital bliss, I spent a long time ruminating about my deficiencies in the art of making marriage truly good. And I resolved to turn over a new leaf and become more giving, more forgiving and more considerate in the hope that Jack would some day talk about me the way that driver had talked about his wife. Instead of thinking of the work I had come to do – a review of projects on cultural heritage preservation – and of the report I had to write, I agonized over my botched telephone conversation with Jack, conjuring up ways to make amends.

Next day, walking down the economy-class aisle (consulting work no longer puts you in business class, which I'm all for in principle but less so in practice), I felt blue at the prospect of lunch and dinner without Jack. However, I was so tired that I was certain I could fall asleep even in a cramped seat, as long as the people next to me were quiet and didn't strike up a conversation. The kind of conversation I dread most during my frequent flights to the Middle East is when, hearing that I grew up in Egypt, people bombard me with all sorts of questions about the region, assuming that I know the answers. As if growing up there qualifies me to answer these impossible questions, such as why women are choosing to wear the *hijab*, or whether the anti-American sentiments there reflect economic problems, or whether Islamism is the consequence of failed nationalism. 'I'm a restorer, a restorer of buildings,' I want to say. 'My work involves the past, not the present.' But I usually let myself be drawn into talking, feeling compelled to say something, no matter how hollow.

The couple next to me looked as grim as I must have that morning. A youngish couple who seemed, fortunately, in no mood for small talk. He sounded Australian and she American. They were arguing with one another over whose fault it was that their one piece of hand luggage was so full that its handle was ripping. The husband was saying that they had gotten carried away at the Khan El Khalili and had bought far too many knick-knacks; the wife maintained they should have bought another suitcase, as they had done on their previous visit to Egypt. We smiled at one another in a perfunctory way, making it clear that none of us expected, or wanted, to socialise.

I'd brought along the *Egyptian Gazette* to read. The crime section invariably grabs my attention, particularly the so-called 'confessions' by apprehended criminals.

While I usually enjoy watching a movie on the plane, however mediocre, that morning I was determined to sleep as much as I could.

The couple – married, I concluded, since both the man and the woman wore wedding rings – continued to argue, still about their Cairene purchases. The woman complained of being pressured by her husband when they were looking at carpets in the Khan El Khalili and of being unable, therefore, to make up her mind; and now she regretted having passed up a carpet that would have been perfect for their living-room. The husband retorted that she need have no regrets as the carpets at that shop were overpriced, and why would she have wanted to buy a carpet from a store that ripped you off?

'Because I like their carpets,' the woman said heatedly. 'So what, if they were slightly more expensive than elsewhere? They were affordable. Much cheaper than anything comparable we can find in London.'

It was not the first time I had experienced people close to me in a plane discussing personal matters so loudly. Perhaps flying uninhibits people and nervousness makes them forget themselves.

'That's not the point,' the husband said.

'So, what is the point?' the woman asked, obviously unwilling to let go.

'I don't like to be ripped off,' he said, then added, 'Do you? – Do you?'

'But what about pleasing me?' she said in a tone that could only stifle any wish on his part to please her.

'Why do you have to turn everything into a test, whether or not I take you into account enough?' he answered calmly.

Apparently ready for this, she shot back: 'Because I would and do consider your preferences. I never, never interfere when you're considering buying something. Do you remember how we spent more than an hour looking at old maps downtown? I've no interest in maps whatsoever but you do, and I was more than happy to let you take your time.'

'Oh, come now. Did this carpet really mean that much to you?' The husband had lost some of his composure.

And on and on the discussion went. I lost interest and closed my eyes. Then I heard nothing. I evidently fell asleep. I was woken by the pilot's announcement: 'Unexpected turbulence over Greece' was the tail end of what I heard. However accustomed I am to flying, turbulence always frightens me. And the turbulence that morning was unusually strong – the plane was shaking so vigorously that the flight attendants abandoned their trolleys and sat down. For a second, the shaking seemed to abate, but then the plane dropped significantly, with a terrifying sensation of falling – and the woman beside me whispered, 'Oh, my God!' I couldn't help looking at her: she was clasping her husband's hand, her head resting against his shoulder. I quickly looked away. I wished I could have held her hand, or anybody's hand. 'Where are you, Jack?' I thought, and then, stupid as it was, I began promising myself and Jack and the Gods out there, that I would never again make a fuss about silly matters. Never. The shaking began again. A man sitting on the other side of the aisle quietly exclaimed 'Damn it!' when his coffee cup spilled on the book he seemed to be still reading. 'How can he read?' I asked myself. The shaking grew so bad that I had to force myself to breathe deeply. That is what Jack would have told me to do. Strange thoughts entered my mind, the strangest being that, if Jack and I had had children, we might have felt towards each other the way that driver felt towards his wife. I heard the pilot tell us to make sure our belts were well fastened, for he was expecting yet more turbulence. His voice sounded stern.

'Honey, I'm sorry I made a fuss about that carpet,' the woman next to me said softly to her husband.

Whatever it was he then whispered back made her say, 'You're so sweet.'

From the corner of my eye, I could see him gently stroking her hair. Still nestled against him and, still clasping his hand, she had closed her eyes. Every time the plane shook particularly badly, the woman said, 'Oh, my God!' and the man said reassuringly, 'It's alright,' or 'Don't worry.' At some point he told her with an apparent certitude that had a calming effect on me too, 'Sweetie, planes don't crash as a result of turbulence,' and she asked, 'Really?,' and he said, 'Really!'

When the turbulence finally stopped – the ten minutes it lasted felt like an eternity – I smiled at the couple, and they smiled back.

'A bit rough,' the man said in a way that suggested he had been tense too, which made me want to tell the woman, 'Forget about the carpet. Your husband's a gem.' There was no need though; she was looking at him with a tenderness that would keep them happy for quite a while now.

The rest of the flight was uneventful. Unable to go back to sleep, I watched the American version of *Shall We Dance*. Much inferior to the original Japanese film, it was perfect viewing for my mood – a mood that told me 'love and be loving to Jack, for this is all that ultimately matters.' The couple next to me watched, holding hands.

After we disembarked I found myself walking behind them. The handle of their hand luggage had completely broken, which made carrying it awkward. It had no wheels. When the woman told the man, 'Well, what did I tell you?' he gave her an exasperated look. Still under the influence of our unsettling experience and still full of good intentions, I had to bite my tongue not to say to them, 'Hey, remember the turbulence!'

Later that evening, when Jack called me to say that he would be a little later than expected because their client wanted to discuss setting up another business, I burst out 'Jack, must you be late tonight, of all nights?'

The turbulence didn't seem to have had, in my case either, too radical an effect, although, after that hasty remark, I did try to be nicer to Jack, ending the call by saying as pleasantly as I could, 'See you darling, when you're done. Take your time.'

Later, waiting for Jack, it occurred to me that I was unlikely now ever to tell him the cab driver's story; that I would remember that story long after the substance of the report I was to start writing in the morning had evaporated from my mind; and that Jack and I would, most probably, spend much of what was left of the evening – once he got home – talking about our work. As I could see where this train of thought was taking me, I told myself – without, however, much conviction – that we were fortunate we enjoyed talking to each other about our work as much as we did.

Next on the List?

After the church service the congregation would gather in the churchyard, unless the day was unusually hot or a *khamsin* was blowing. A much-esteemed member of the congregation – esteemed for the money he had, not for his piousness or benevolence – was an elderly, small and rotund, ruddy gentleman who had a pronounced tendency to blush scarlet at the slightest annoyance. This man never lingered much in the churchyard; yet he made his presence felt by barking orders to his entourage, a wife, brothers and sisters, brothers-in-law, sisters-in-law, nephews and nieces, grandchildren, as well as great-nephews and great-nieces. An almost perpetual look of amusement on his wife's face suggested that she did not take him too seriously. But everyone else in his entourage seemed on edge.

The rotund gentleman – the smallest of the men in his retinue – was evidently looked on as the family patriarch, though he was not the eldest. Not that the other men in the family were nobodies; but they could not match the fortune he had amassed through fair and, some hinted, foul means. So everybody, even the more recalcitrant members of the family, ultimately deferred to him. He was not wholly objectionable. He was smart and vivacious, could be very witty and even generous occasionally; he was not mean, he was just unabashedly egotistic. For that reason, and because of all the money he had – enough money to do things on his own terms and buy people off as he pleased – many found him insufferable.

Ordering people about, talking with vehemence and much gesticulation, and nodding his head in all directions in acknowledgement of greetings, the gentleman would cross the churchyard very slowly. Once on the pavement he would stop. To beggars, he gave sparingly. With snack vendors, he drove hard bargains, after which he would look for his car – a big old American car – and would invariably curse the driver for parking it in the wrong spot, no matter where it was parked. Sometimes those walking closest to him would hear him tell his wife, if she happened to be close by, 'Oh! I wish we were alone. I wish I didn't have to put up with all these people,' to which she usually replied, 'Come now, don't get overwrought: you know full well that you love having a large following.'

As might be expected, he had his favourites of the moment – both amongst the adults and the children, and did not hide his preferences very well, although he put on a show of fairness. On Sundays, just before climbing into his car, he routinely gave some pocket money to his grandchildren, great-nephews and great-nieces, making a point of apportioning the money equally, though according to their respective ages. The older ones got more than the younger ones. To the older boys he usually gave the most, on the basis that they needed more money to take their girlfriends out, although he sometimes favoured the older girls, telling them,

'I know you girls! You like to spend money on making yourselves look pretty.'

For people like this elderly gentleman, the early sixties were a tumultuous time in Egypt. As far as rich people were concerned, Nasser – Egypt's young, handsome and charismatic leader – was a dangerous man on the rampage, as shown by his escalating attacks on their wealth and privileges. At the time this story was unfolding, the government had already begun confiscating private property. 'Nationalisation' and 'sequestration' were the order of the day. For the rich, these were naturally much dreaded words. The regime kept them in suspense: whose turn would it be next?

This political turn of events was giving the elderly gentleman at the centre of this story even more reasons to get red in the face, display irritation and boss people around. The fact that he and his peers were losing their possessions, as well as overall control of the country, seemed to make him keener than ever to control his entourage and assert his authority.

Grandchildren, great-nephews and great-nieces saw him at his worst during that turbulent period. Never particularly popular with them, despite the money he gave them, his popularity sank to even lower levels as his temper flared up more and more frequently and his imperiousness touched new heights.

One of his great-nephews, a lanky adolescent, had come to dislike him with a passion. The boy was the son of one of the rich man's many nieces. In the rich man's opinion, and, to be fair, the opinion of just about every family member, this young woman had committed a folly by marrying an outsider, a Jew rumoured to be a member of the Communist party at the time of the marriage.

The marriage had been short-lived, exactly as the rich uncle had predicted. The outsider had left wife, son and country and gone to Paris.

This had all happened before 1956, before the Jewish exodus from Egypt. To his wife the husband had said that he was leaving because her family was making his life miserable, which they were. To friends, however, he had apparently said that he was leaving because the signs were that Egypt and Israel would come to blows: he was uneasy living in Egypt with that possibility looming. Once in Paris he had tried to stay in touch with his son, but was led to understand by members of his wife's family that the boy would be better off left alone. Complying with their wishes, he disappeared altogether from the scene.

'Good riddance,' the rich man had told the family and even the young wife, inconsolable and penniless. Her husband had had a job but no money, another reason why her family had disapproved of the marriage. His leaving had made her dependent on her father, an inveterate gambler who had squandered much of his inheritance and was subsisting on a tiny pension in addition to the meagre rental income from a small building he owned in Abdeen, one of Cairo's old and dilapidated neighbourhoods. In the end the young woman had had to work, teaching French at a couple of schools and tutoring on the side. Every so often her rich uncle, as well as other well-off uncles and aunts, would give her some money, which she accepted without any show of protest.

Thus the boy had grown up in modest, though by no means uncomfortable, circumstances. He hardly ever thought of his father. He identified so little with his Jewish lineage that when the tone at school, especially in his social science classes, became anti-Zionist, often bordering on anti-Jewish, he felt relatively unconcerned. Sometimes, though, he did wonder how his school friends would react were they ever to find out about his Jewish father. They were under the impression that he was of Syro-Lebanese origins, on both his father's side and his mother's side. The rare times he gave the matter any thought, it angered him that this absent father of his could still end up being a liability in his life.

Not surprisingly the boy was a very private and quiet sort – on the taciturn side. He was far too private and quiet for his rich great-uncle's liking. The elderly man did not have an especially negative opinion of the boy. It was more that the boy disconcerted him – a feeling he did not like. So his response was not to pay him too much attention.

More or less ignored by his great-uncle, the boy grew to loathe him, observing with distaste how little money he gave to beggars, how he bargained whenever he bought anything, how he shouted his requests instead of asking politely, how he seemed to enjoy making scenes. The boy had no trouble finding countless flaws in the man; and he came to feel his connection to him as embarrassing and humiliating. And yet, whenever the old man gave him his pocket money, he would open his hand, take the money and mumble a barely audible and reluctant 'thank you', all the time wanting the earth to swallow him up.

Each Sunday meeting brought a repetition of this money-giving ritual, followed by an excruciatingly tedious family lunch at the great-uncle's house – a lunch at which all the adults seemed to feel compelled to offer rapturous praise for each dish served. During these lunches the boy would make a point of eating conspicuously little in the vain hope that, some day, the master of the house would notice his abstemiousness. But his great-uncle had other things on his mind. He never seemed to notice how little the boy ate. If he ever did, he never remarked upon it.

Shortly after his twelfth birthday, the boy's resentment of his great-uncle turned into a wish to see the old man humbled somehow. At first, that thought – most present in the boy's mind just before the Sunday family get-togethers – was shapeless. But it took a more definite form the day he began hearing some boys at school – the sons of highly placed officials in the new regime – give the names of companies and wealthy men that would appear, they claimed, on the next list of nationalisations and sequestrations.

One Sunday, during one of the tedious, nerve-racking lunches to which he had been subjected ever since he was a little boy, he saw an opportunity to try out his idea. No sooner had the lunch started than his great-uncle launched into an attack on the new regime. 'A gang of inept thieves,' he thundered, and then proceeded to dissect the regime's policies. Present at that lunch were two members of the old regime, including an ex-minister. While the great-uncle went on and on, the two guests were observing, out of the corner of their eyes, the house servant standing at attention in the dining room. They were wondering whether it was safe for their host to be speaking in front of the house servant, for one never knew, these days, who might report what to whom. Noticing their unease, their hostess put their minds at ease, assuring them that she could vouch for the man's loyalty: he had been in their service for over thirty years, he considered them family. Thus reassured, the two gentlemen took turns to expatiate on the real and supposed evils of the new regime.

As soon as the gentlemen were finished with their tirades, the boy, now seated at the table for grown-ups, decided to seize the moment to do what he had been secretly wanting to do for some time. He leaned towards his mother and whispered something in her ear. That something led her to exclaim 'Oh! No!', which, naturally, caught the attention of the master of the house.

'What is it?' his great-uncle asked with a tone that suggested that the only displays of emotion he tolerated at his table were his own.

'Nothing, uncle, nothing, really!' the boy's mother said nervously.

'It cannot be nothing, Lina! You wouldn't have been taken aback if it were nothing. Now, you tell me what this boy of yours whispered in your ear! It must be of some interest – he rarely opens his mouth.'

So, his great-uncle had actually noticed him whispering to his mother, the boy noted with excitement!

'Well,' she said with some hesitation, 'why don't I let him tell you. I'm not sure that I got it right.'

'So what do you have to tell us, young gentleman?' the great-uncle shouted from his far end of the table. 'You don't usually say much.'

The boy lowered his eyes and said softly, 'I was just telling Mother that I heard some boys at school say that your name will appear on the next list.'

'On what list?' the great-uncle screamed, sounding stupefied, although he had guessed, of course, what list the boy was talking about.

There was a deathly hush in the room. All eyes were suddenly on the boy, including those of the house servant, who was in the midst of recirculating the first course.

'The list of sequestrations,' the boy said with unusual assertiveness, now looking straight at his great-uncle.

'Nonsense!' the great-uncle yelled. 'Pure and utter nonsense! I have my connections! They would not dare!' And, crimson in the face, he angrily turned his eyes away from the boy.

The look of perpetual amusement on his wife's face vanished. She looked grim now. Noticing that both guests were shaking their heads with an air of consternation, the house servant hurriedly offered them more of the first course, a dish of potatoes au gratin.

Nobody dared reopen the dreadful subject.

At first it seemed to the boy that his fabricated but plausible story had missed the mark. Yet, as the lunch progressed, the fact that his great-uncle was relatively subdued suggested to him that it might have had some effect – not enough though. He had hoped for something more dramatic. He had hoped to elicit a reaction from his great-uncle that would reveal the man as powerless and vulnerable. That had not happened.

After lunch, when his mother announced that she had to hurry home because she had to give a lesson, even though it was Sunday – a case of helping a mediocre student with last-minute cramming for an exam – his great-uncle walked them to the door. This was unprecedented. Never before had his great-uncle bothered accompanying them to the door. His mother was surprised and embarrassed. He suspected that it had something to do with his little lunchtime performance.

'Are you sure you heard my name mentioned?' the great-uncle asked him at the door in a muted voice.

'I think so,' the boy replied, putting on an air of concern. For a brief moment, the boy and the old man looked each other straight in the eye. They were more or less the same height. During that brief moment the great-uncle no longer seemed daunting to the boy. He suddenly looked like any old man. The boy felt a tinge of guilt, immediately killed when he quickly remembered the man's overbearing ways.

'Well,' the great-uncle finally said, more softly than the boy had ever heard him speak, 'will you, please, double-check for me?'

A wonderful feeling of satisfaction surged up within the boy. His great-uncle was asking him for a favour and had even said 'please'! What a victory! Then, patting the boy's cheek, the old man promised, 'You'll get a reward for your efforts, some money, more than usual.' The boy hung his head, once again full of loathing for the old man.

The next day at school the boy volunteered his services to raise Egypt's flag before the assembled student body, and to lead the chorus of 'Long live the United Arab Republic' chanting that took place, every morning, before classes started. Because his social background was too old-regime and too Westernised, he was uncertain whether he would end up amongst the chosen few to whom this task was regularly delegated. But, at least, he would have tried.

He has Aged

John Harman had flown from Chicago to Amsterdam, given a talk and stayed overnight, then, at the crack of dawn, on to London for another talk and, a couple of hours after that, on to Cairo to catch a train to go to Luxor. In less than three days he had been catapulted from blustery, cold Chicago to sunny Luxor. It was March. An archaeologist, in theory he was in Luxor to size up the prospects of a dig. In reality, he wanted time to breathe. His marriage had become a war zone, to the point where hardly a word was uttered without hostility and defensiveness, on both his and his wife's parts. This had been going on for at least three years. Before that there had been tensions but also the occasional good times. Now there was only acrimony.

He was past trying to figure out what had gone wrong in a marriage that had looked promising at the outset. His few-and-far-between flings, which his wife sensed? Hers, whose existence he sometimes doubted, as she seemed to throw them right in his face, clearly to pique his jealousy? All he wanted now was to get out of the marriage in a decent fashion, but that was unlikely, since the bitterness between them had reached massive proportions. To think that they had promised each other, when they got married, that they would never sink to the level of mutual recriminations and, should things not work out, they would call it quits before the marriage got ugly! Yet, still married, they were mired in ugliness. Their three children, ranging in age from fifteen to twenty-one, all assumed that it was only a matter of time till one of them walked out. The older two had let it be known that they were thoroughly fed up with their parents' scenes.

So, approached to give the conferences in Amsterdam and London, John had jumped at the opportunity to get away, and had tacked on the trip to Luxor. His wife, an epidemiologist, did a fair amount of travelling herself, mostly in Asia and Latin America. They had both been successful in their professions, which should have helped their marriage, but it had not.

Luxor was a bit like home for him: he had been coming here for years. He still loved it in spite of the hordes of tourists who had started to return after a two-year lull following the terrorist attack in the Hatchseput temple. March was a good month to be in Luxor, warm without being really hot, and relatively quiet.

He stayed at the Pharaohs, on the west bank of the Nile. The hotel was close to Medinet Habu, his favourite complex of funerary temples. Set apart from the other monuments, Medinet Habu was not overrun by tourists. There were times in the afternoons when you could wander through the temples and be by yourself. In the evenings, if you bribed the guards to let you in after-hours, you were guaranteed peace and quiet. Then, the magic of the site would grip you. He was counting on that feeling to bring back traces of his former, better self. In Medinet Habu he hoped he would put his marital problems and even his flings, about which he did feel sheepish, out of his mind. When he dwelt on his unfaithfulness he told himself that the fleeting nature of these furtive encounters – that had meant so little and served only as an escape – should absolve him from too much guilt, though he knew this would introduce another guilt, towards the women involved. It would have been simpler had he fallen in love. One would have thought that he would be seeking happiness elsewhere, when his marriage turned really sour. Oddly though, his constant anxiety about the marriage left little room for love. Casual pleasure was another thing.

Some years earlier Luxor had been the scene of one of his amorous encounters. The woman was staying at the Habu House, the older of the two hotels within walking distance of Medinet Habu: a whitewashed mud-brick building with a lovely roof garden, Habu House had both more charm than the Pharaohs and more insects, with the occasional scorpion, and fewer amenities. He had met her in the garden, at a time when the problems in his marriage were becoming obvious.

More than the woman herself, he remembered what he had thought of her: that she must have been gutsy to be travelling alone. Ursula was her name. A Danish woman from Copenhagen. In her early thirties. Neither particularly attractive nor unattractive. Reserved yet adventurous, and with a thirst for exotica that had quickly got on his nerves.

This time he would avoid romance. He wanted distance from all that was painful. Any romance would remind him of the failure of his marriage.

After he had checked in, he slept for much of the day, but only after the usual long chat with the hotel's owner, whose father, a doorman in Cairo, had started the business.

In the evening, he walked to Medinet Habu. The guards – a new set of guards – refused the bribe he offered to be let in to the complex after hours: they knew him and simply let him in. It was, they said, his first day back in Luxor, and he deserved a treat.

He was on excellent terms with the locals – the tourist guides, the inspectors, the sheikhs who led the teams of excavators, the excavators who sometimes worked as guides, the temple guards, and even the children who chased the tourists. They all seemed to like him. A sure sign was to be invited for meals at someone's home. Over the years he had been invited for wonderful and copious meals by several different local families – well-off and humble families.

He skipped going to the hotel's café/bar and went to bed early that first day. The hotel was fuller than he had anticipated.

The next morning, up very early, he revised his lecture notes in light of the questions asked at the end of his London and Amsterdam talks. He did this in the hotel garden.

Around nine in the morning, before it got hot, he climbed up and over the shoulder of the Gurn, then down along a winding path, into the Valley of the Kings. Tourists were already swarming over the temples. Local guides, inspectors and guards greeted him warmly, expressing the wish that he stay for some time. This seemed an excellent idea: he ought to consider undertaking some major project in Luxor – an excavation, an epigraphic survey or perhaps the restoration of a temple. Something that would keep him in Luxor for a long while, away from Chicago and his life there.

He spent the morning roaming around the temples and talking to government employees.

He had lunch at the Pharaohs, a Greek cheese sandwich, olives and an orange: to be safe, he avoided greens and tomatoes.

In the afternoon he walked to Medinet Habu, lay on a stone in the shade and had a nap. The guards did not disturb him. He dreamed that he was with his children, in the Cairo Museum.

That evening he went to the Pharaoh's café/bar. Not much of a drinker, he enjoyed an occasional cold beer – a Stella – particularly if it was served with fresh-tasting peanuts. As soon as he entered the room, a group of three young, handsome Egyptian men seated in one corner, sipping tea, spotted him, got up and called over to him. He had known the three men, Omar, Tarek and Ali, since they were adolescents. Now, they were grown-up men in their late twenties. Omar and Tarek were married and had children. Ali had already acquired the reputation of being a confirmed bachelor, though his mother had not given up on finding him a suitable wife. The three worked as freelance tourist guides and excavators, depending on the season and the availability of jobs. They were hard-working, lively and quick-witted, with many good jokes to tell about the Supreme Council for Antiquities and about Cairenes in general. They had grown up together, and behaved like brothers. Used to his colleagues' competitive ways, John Harman was still surprised, even after years of spending time in Egypt, at the relative lack of competitiveness amongst Egyptian men. It was, he thought, an appealing trait.

He embraced each one of the three young men: it turned out they had been waiting for him. They had heard that he had arrived in Luxor and was staying, as usual, at the Pharaohs. The three were smoking and, though they knew he did not smoke, out of politeness they offered him a cigarette. He told them that his cigarette days were definitely over, but he would gladly have some mint tea. They wouldn't have minded his having a beer, but he thought it more courteous to drink tea, since they were drinking tea.

In English and with the occasional word or phrase in Arabic, the conversation began with chat about the Supreme Council for Antiquities, and the new directives it was issuing – in the young men's opinion, all misguided. The question of the appointment of new temple guards also cropped up and the odd ways the new appointees had secured their jobs.

'I hope your wife and children are in good health,' Omar said to John.

'They are doing well, thank God. And how are Samiha and the children?' he inquired.

'Samiha is Samiha. You know her. Always worrying about the children. Too much! Hamada goes to school now. He's a big boy.'

'And how's your mother? Better?' Tarek asked John.

That Tarek remembered his mother's heart problems touched John.

'Much, much better, thank God,' John said. 'And how is your father? How is his back?'

'He's getting old, but he thinks he's young,' Tarek said.

The four men laughed.

John was thinking that Tarek's father was not so old. Only in his sixties. Yet, to Tarek, Omar and Ali he was an old man. Did he too seem like an old man to them? He wondered how they viewed a man about to turn fifty.

'Did you hear about the new rules for getting excavation

permits?' Ali asked John in a tone that spoke volumes of what he thought of them.

'I don't think so,' John said, careful to sound neutral. He was well aware that, while the young men relished criticising their government, they might take offence, if he, a foreigner, did the same.

'Ali, don't upset John tonight by telling him about those crazy rules. Let's have more mint tea,' Tarek interjected. 'This isn't the time to get upset; let's be happy.'

Ali, however, did not drop the subject of excavations, asking John, 'Do you plan to do excavation work soon?'

The thought crossed John's mind that Ali might be looking for work. He was a great employee. Reliable and eager to work long hours, as long as the pay was good. Some said Ali was greedy. John had employed him a couple of times and had been happy with his performance.

'Perhaps,' John answered. 'I'll certainly let you know if I do.'

'I hope you do, then you'll be staying with us for a while,' Ali said, apparently genuine.

'So you must have met the new guards at Medinet Habu!' Omar stated, with an edge in his voice.

John knew that the new senior guard came from a family that had had feuds with Omar's family. 'I did,' he said, refraining from offering any comment. He didn't much mind the new guard, though was none too keen on his parents, with whom he had had some dealings.

'We'll see what happens to Medinet Habu now,' Omar said ominously.

The four men were quiet. Tarek's and Ali's families were on

reasonable terms with the new guard's family. There was some awkwardness in the air. But it did not last long as Ali suddenly pulled out a big, brown envelope from his *galabeyah*'s pockets and took from it a thick bundle of letters.

'John,' he said, 'will you help me? Can you read some letters for me? You know I speak English better than I read it. It's alright if the words are printed, but letters written by hand are very difficult to read.'

Omar pulled out a few letters from his shirt pocket and laughed, 'I need some help too.'

Tarek said, 'Thank God, I have no letters to show! They do, but I don't!' And he repeated, 'Thank God,' half-jokingly, half-seriously, it seemed to John.

Ali was the first to hand a letter to John. It said:

November 16, 2000

Sweetest Ali,

When, oh when, will I be back in Luxor? I can't wait to be with you. Life in Liverpool is so drab. No laughter, no sun, no warmth, and no Ali! At work, my girl friends ask me, with envy, about my Egyptian love story, though they think it's a passing thing. I don't bother explaining to them that it is serious, that you are the man for me, and you make me feel I am the woman for you.

The men I have known before you (I won't hide that I have known a few men, even though I know you have a jealous streak) were so bland. You're so full of life. I will do all I can to come for Christmas. I need you. I hope you need me too! Anything you want me to bring along? Anything you want me to send you, if I hear of people going to Luxor?

Don't hesitate to tell me. I know that life is a struggle for you, and for your family, and yet you all keep your spirits up and are so cheerful!

Yours always,

Rhonda

Before John could say anything, Ali thrust another letter in his hand:

Darling Ali,

I shall never, never forget the ten days we spent together in Luxor. They were, thanks to you, so incredibly good. If only I could find a way of spending part of the year in Luxor! It would be great! Ideally, I would want to spend at least December, January and February in Luxor, with you of course, and, who knows, I might find ways of bringing you over here, though I am sure that you would miss Egypt and your family terribly. Life in Philadelphia is nothing like the life you're used to. Things follow such a set routine here. It gets me down horribly. I would be worried that you would lose your beautiful smile here.

Don't forget your Ingrid.

Then, a third letter:

January 2001

Sunny Ali,

I'm going crazy. It's pitch-dark when I go to work. And pitch-dark when I return. I spend lunchtime in an overheated cafeteria. It hasn't stopped raining for one month. Yes, one whole month! When I get home at night, I play the Um Kulsum tape you gave me. I don't understand the words. But it's not important since I know she sings about 'Hubb'. Love! Love! Love! Love you, sweetie!!! I realise that to talk about love, after spending only a few days with someone, seems ridiculous but my heart tells me I love you and you have to listen to what your heart says. Don't you? The two weeks we spent together in Luxor taught me so much about love.

Time in Liverpool drags on and on …

Do you need anything?

Many, many kisses.

Your 'Basbusa'

'What exactly did you do to these ladies?' John asked Ali, and the two men laughed good-heartedly.

'They are nice ladies,' Ali answered without any shyness. 'They seem so alone. Life seems hard for them. They work hard. They don't spend time with their families. They are at home alone in the evenings. They travel alone. I don't understand. They are good ladies.'

Tarek joked, 'Ali is a Don Juan, but Omar is one too.' Then, turning to Omar, Tarek said in Arabic, 'Shame on you, man. You have a wife and children.' Then, turning to John, he continued in English, 'You must tell Omar to be good. Samiha is a good wife.' This was said in good humour but with a touch of seriousness that John found endearing.

'Now you can read my letters,' Omar told John. 'I don't have many. Then you can go back to Ali's letters. He's a bigger Don Juan than I am. He has more time than I do.'

Omar was definitely the most handsome of the three young men. Tall, broad-shouldered, with high cheekbones, fiery black eyes under bushy eyebrows, full lips, a large forehead and bushy jet black hair. Lovely hands too. A pianist's hands that were much in evidence when he played the tabla – he played it well.

The letter he handed to John read:

January 2001

My dearest,

I fell in love with your country the first time I visited it. It was eight years ago. I absolutely loved it, in particular Luxor. Getting to know it through your eyes has made me even fonder of it. No man managed to make me appreciate a place the way you have. There are plenty of 'experts' who go to Egypt, but they don't really know it. They know it with their head. That's all and that's not enough. I realise that you are not a free man. You have a wife and children. I admire you for telling me about them. You did not pretend you were a free man. As you know, I come to Luxor often. I have become addicted to the place. I am willing to spend time with you on your terms! I promise not to interfere with your family life. I know family is very important to you, even if you are not happy in your marriage.

Should I come around Easter time? The heat does not bother me. In fact, I like the heat.

If you can write a few words back, you'll make me very happy.

Your Ulla,

or Olla as you nicknamed me. I love the sound of Olla It is so much nicer than Ursula, a name I always hated. I keep your real Olla in my kitchen, and drink water from it every morning. It connects me to Luxor and to you.

'Could it be the same Ursula from Copenhagen I had a fling

with?' was John's immediate thought. 'Ursula's not so common a name.'

He looked at Omar. He saw a man twenty years younger than himself. A man belonging to a totally different world than his, who might have slept with a woman he had slept with. 'So what?' he tried to tell himself. If he was entitled to have his flings, so was Omar. 'But the bastard was likely after her money!' he caught himself thinking. And was surprised at the strong wave of hostility welling up within him, and at his sudden dislike of Omar, and of Ali too, for that matter. He could not help thinking that the Omars and Alis of the world had no business playing games with the Ursulas, Jeans and Rhondas of the world. But what about his own behaviour? It was not as though he himself had behaved well towards his Ursula. He had asked for her address, had jotted it down on a piece of paper, without meaning ever to get in touch. He remembered now giving her his work e-mail address. She had sent him a brief message he had not even bothered to acknowledge. He always made sure that his flings never got out of hand.

'Have you finished reading it?' Omar asked him eagerly.

'Yes, yes,' John replied.

'Can you help me answer, when you have time?'

'Hey, Omar, you're a married man, as Tarek says,' John said, trying to sound light-hearted. 'What would Samiha think about all this?'

'That's what I've been saying to him,' Tarek exclaimed.

'You're just envious,' Ali and Omar said in unison to Tarek. 'Admit it!'

'Omar, what you're doing is not right,' Tarek said gently. Then in English, to John, he said, 'Don't you think so?'

John nodded. He was wondering whether to ask Omar where his Ursula came from – what country, what city. 'Better not to find out though,' he concluded. There were many Ursulas in the world, many in Copenhagen.

'You seem tired,' Ali observed with concern. 'We have tired you. What time is it in Chicago now?'

John handed him the letter. 'Yes, you're right. I am tired. It's the time difference. Stopping in Amsterdam and London to give talks didn't help. I'll go to bed very early tonight.'

After that, the subject of the letters was dropped. Sensing John's unease, Omar and Ali returned to talking about the Supreme Council for Antiquities. It was not long before John got up and wished the men goodnight. After hugging each one of them, he bought himself a bottle of beer to take to his room.

'He has aged,' Omar said.

'You think he took offence because of the letters?' Tarek wondered.

'He might feel we should not get too close to their women. But is it our fault, if they come here desperate for love? And for some tenderness?' Ali lit another cigarette.

'God be my witness, I felt sorry for this Olla. She's the one who chased me,' Omar said.

'Come on, brother! You did not have to go along! You're not behaving properly towards Samiha,' Tarek stated.

'You're right,' Omar admitted, and he looked suddenly subdued.

'Do you think he'll help us reply?' Ali asked.

'He's a good sort. He probably will,' Omar said.

Back in his room, John stretched on his bed, his nerves all jangled. He must be more tired than he thought. All seemed suddenly sordid to him, his life as well as Luxor. His belligerent feelings towards Omar were subsiding. It was not news to him that some Western women came to Luxor in search of some sort of love. He had known about that side of life in Luxor. Wasn't this what the Ursula he had met had been looking for? And hadn't he taken advantage of that? Still, the thought of Omar's intimacy with her did not go down well with him. Whether or not his Ursula was in fact Omar's 'Olla' he would never know.

Trying to make light of it all, he told himself, 'Omar is a more handsome man than I am' – an understatement, as Omar was much, much more handsome than him.

For the first time, in a long while, John wondered whether his marriage could be salvaged.

I Want These Pills

Nora and her mother seemed locked in a struggle of wills of the kind that normally pits a young girl against her mother – except that Nora was forty-six years old and her mother eighty-eight. The argument was taking place in the old lady's bedroom at nine in the evening, just as Nora was thinking that she ought to start packing her suitcase, as she had to be at the airport at the crack of dawn next day. She was on the eve of returning home – home for her being Montreal and thus miles away from Cairo, where her ailing mother lived.

The week she had spent in Cairo had been frantic, like all her recent stays in Cairo. Her last couple of trips had been particularly taxing as she had been confronted, from the minute she set foot in her mother's apartment, with a long list of things to do. Despite having a housekeeper and two part-time carers, her increasingly frail mother needed all the help she could get to carry on living at home. The elderly lady did not want to move into a nursing home. Nora did not want her there either, and so was doing her best to lend a helping hand by visiting her more frequently, squeezing in as many errands as she could during her brief visits, and making sure the carers were happy but not idle. Nora's handling of her mother's affairs required tact and deft manoeuvring: it was important that her mother should not be made to feel so diminished as to be powerless. Though very frail, the old lady had retained her intellectual vigour and mental acuity. She was not a difficult person, although, of late, she could become inordinately preoccupied by small matters, and then would not let go of her preoccupation. Whenever that happened, she became a different person from the measured and sensible woman whom people were used to.

It would have made everything so much easier were Nora's mother living in Montreal, or Nora living in Cairo. However, Nora's family and job were in Montreal. Her mother had lived all her life in Cairo. To uproot her, at this stage, would be, to say the least, problematical. Nora had given the matter some thought and reached the conclusion that the present arrangement, though not ideal, was more manageable than transplanting her mother to a new world so late in life. The matter had never been put on the table though: her mother herself had never raised the subject.

A couple of months had elapsed between Nora's last visit and this one. Over so short a time, the old lady's health had visibly deteriorated. There was no single cause for this: it was a generalised decline, which had taken Nora by surprise. On the phone her mother had sounded in good health; face-to-face she appeared about to break, so frail had she become.

Nora was her only child. There had been a son who had died in a car crash at the age of twenty-eight. Nora and her mother rarely spoke of him. It seemed to Nora that her mother had never much wanted to share her grief.

During the week of frantic errands for her mother, just about every day Nora would ask herself 'How am I going to manage to say goodbye this time?' On the day she was to fly back to Montreal, this was on her mind all day long.

Completely saturated with taking and giving instructions, going over old lists and making new ones, Nora was hoping that, right after she had finished packing, she would have time to sit down with her mother and have a leisurely talk, as had been their habit in the past, on the eve of her leaving. But her mother had other plans. She had made up her mind that she needed a certain kind of antibiotic, for which she happened to have an old prescription. She wanted Nora to go to the pharmacy to pick it up.

Gently, Nora tried to dissuade her mother from getting the medication: 'But why get this antibiotic now? You don't know whether you have an infection. I didn't hear you complain about any symptoms earlier in the day.'

Already in bed, her mother replied in a tone that made it clear she did not consider the matter to be open to discussion, 'I may not start taking them today. But I want them handy.'

'I don't think it's advisable for you to take them without having some tests first,' Nora suggested. 'Besides, I noticed that you tend to take antibiotics without completing the whole course. That's not good, Mother. You're too casual about this.'

'Oh!' her mother exclaimed, and turned her face away from Nora. 'At my age, does it matter? Please, go to the pharmacy now, before it's too late!'

'Mother, I see no reason to get these pills now! I'm against your self-medicating yourself that way. Knowing you, you will take them, then stop mid-course.' Why she was adopting this superior tone was not clear to Nora; but she had, and was now carried along by it. The expression on her face mirrored the self-righteous tone.

Her mother did not answer, slowly got out of bed, and put on her slippers and house-coat.

'Bewildered, Nora asked her sharply, 'What are you doing?'

Again without answering, her mother walked out of the bedroom. Following her, Nora almost shouted, 'But where are you going?'

With a blank look her mother answered: 'Since you're not willing to go to the pharmacy, I'll ask a neighbour to go for me.'

'This is ridiculous!' Nora screamed, past trying to be gentle. 'Why not wait till tomorrow? Till you have the tests? Talk to the doctor first thing in the morning, and then, if he thinks you need the pills, Soad can get them for you.'

With astonishing force for someone so frail, the elderly lady barked at Nora, 'You go now! I want these pills!'

Nora was dumbfounded. It was uncharacteristic of her mother to be giving – let alone shouting – orders. 'I won't go! It makes no sense to get them now. You shouldn't be taking pills on a whim.' This time Nora managed to avoid screaming, but the look she threw in her mother's direction was brimming with hostility.

Her mother walked towards the apartment's entrance door.

'It's nine o'clock, Mother!' Nora was shouting again. And, even louder, 'It makes no sense! No sense whatsoever!' She sat down in the livingroom, hung her head, and put her hands first on her forehead and then on her cheeks. She could feel her cheeks burning. 'My face must be all red,' she thought. Her neck and shoulders felt like one big knot.

When Nora saw her mother walk back to her bedroom a few minutes later, she did not ask her whether the neighbours would get her the pills. Without uttering a word, her mother went straight back to bed, although she did not lie down. She propped herself against her pillows and sat with the same empty look she had had at the height of their argument.

Nora joined her and sat on the bed, thinking that may be now was the time to have their leisurely talk, although it did not look promising. 'So,' Nora asked, 'will you be going out a bit this week?'

'Perhaps,' her mother answered without looking at Nora.

'I wonder what will be waiting for me at work,' Nora stated, hoping that this would capture her mother's interest.

Ignoring Nora's question, her mother said, 'I've just remembered that I've been wanting you to check the silverware in the safe, and also to find the second key to the safe. I seem to have misplaced it.'

'Now?' Nora exclaimed.

'Yes.'

'Mother, you can't be serious! Do you realise that I'm leaving at dawn tomorrow morning?' Nora shook her head.

'I do! I do! The last thing I need is for you to remind me! That's why I'm asking you to do it now,' her mother cried, sounding suddenly panicky. Really panicky.

'But why didn't you tell me earlier?' Nora looked furious.

'I only just remembered now! What do you expect at my age?' her mother said, more calmly. 'You should be glad I'm managing as well as I am. It could be worse, you know!'

'Frankly Mother, you don't seem to allow for the fact that I'm getting up at four-thirty tomorrow morning,' Nora said, although what she really wanted to say was 'I would like to talk with you Mother, the way we usually do – the way we've not had much of a chance to, this time round.'

The elderly lady looked as if she was about to reply, but did not.

Relentless, Nora continued: 'Why suddenly the concern for the silverware?' She was very tempted to point out 'You're not about to use it soon,' but restrained herself. 'And why worry about this second key? Why?'

Her mother raised her eyebrows and said, with a touch of irony in her voice, 'I like to know where my keys are.'

'Look,' Nora said gruffly, 'I'll pack first, and then, if I feel up to it, I'll check the silverware and try to find the key.'

As she got up Nora was surprised to see the expression on her mother's face grow slightly more relaxed. She said, 'I might be asleep by then.'

'So we'll talk in the morning,' Nora suggested.

'You can't count on my being alert at four-thirty in the morning,' her mother said.

Frowning, Nora replied, 'Well then, we'll talk when I call you from Montreal. And, if I find the key, I'll leave it on your little writing desk, but don't count on it. I'm exhausted.'

'If I'm not up in the morning, have a safe trip,' her mother said. 'Now, would you switch off the light?'

Nora kissed her, switched off the light and left the room, noticing that her mother had not wished her a good night.

'But why, oh why, should the week end on that terrible note?'

Nora wondered as she started packing her suitcase. After she had finished she found the missing key, but was too tired to check the silverware.

The night was short but felt very long for Nora. She hardly slept. She heard her mother get up several times. For part of the night, there was a light in her mother's bedroom. Nora thought of going in to check but decided that she could not face her mother staring into space, or looking agitated. Tomorrow the carers would take over. As far as she was concerned she had done all she could during her fleeting one-week stay but, evidently, it was not enough. The fridge, the curtains and the rugs needed cleaning. Some faucets were leaking. One of the armchairs needed re-upholstering. The sad thing was that her mother, who used to attach enormous significance to how the apartment looked, did not seem to mind or notice its dingy state.

At some point during that interminable night, Nora asked herself whether it was really out of the question to have her mother move to Montreal. She asked herself this in the abstract, knowing, deep down, that she would not feel up to handling her mother on top of her job, her husband and her daughters.

Meanwhile, in her bedroom, the old lady alternated between staring into space, reading, dozing, getting up to go to the bathroom, and going over an account book in which she kept a meticulous record of her expenses. She both dreaded and wanted the morning to come; both dreaded and wanted her daughter to leave, since such leaving was inevitable. Now that she really needed her daughter, her daughter's brief stays agitated her. Now she found it easier to express her emotions from a distance. Perhaps she had got used to the distance, to living her life alone

and far away from her daughter. There was no question in her mind that living close to her daughter and grandchildren would have been infinitely preferable. But that was not meant to be.

At times like these she could not help but think of the son who had died such an untimely death. 'A mother who survives the death of a child can survive any absence,' she thought. Then, 'I cannot let emotions take hold of me. If I do, then what?' and she forced herself to read, which she did for quite a while until thoughts of her own mother crept into her mind. She remembered how frustrating she had found it to look after her mother after the ailing lady had moved in with her. She remembered how self-absorbed her mother had become at the end of her life. She feared becoming like her mother.

At five o'clock Nora tiptoed into her mother's bedroom. She stood by the bed, hoping her mother would sense her presence; but she seemed to be sleeping. Nora whispered, 'Mother, I'm leaving.' With her eyes closed, her mother replied softly, 'Have a safe trip, darling; call me, as soon as you get home, to let me know all is well.'

'I will,' Nora assured her, then gave her a light kiss on the head and quietly left the room.

In the cab taking her to the airport at a frightening speed, Nora was resentful that her mother had not made the effort to sit up and have tea with her. At the terminal, waiting at the gate to embark, she thought of calling her, then changed her mind, telling herself, 'What's the point? I've done all I can do.'

When Nora called her mother from Montreal the first thing she said to her was, 'Mother, would you consider moving to Montreal to live with us?' then waited for the answer with apprehension.

For a few seconds, there was silence on the line, then her mother said, 'It's too late really; too late!' There was silence again, then her mother added, 'I doubt that it would be any easier in Montreal. You know how Grandma got to be at the end of her life. Her living with us did not prevent her from becoming both depressed and difficult. I wouldn't want to put you through that, darling, but I appreciate your raising the subject. Besides, I'm managing. Not too badly, I think.' Ashamed of her unmistakeable sense of relief, Nora replied, her voice faltering, 'I care a lot, a lot. I wish things could be different.' Her mother, comforting her by saying 'Stop worrying, darling; it will all work out,' gave her the absolution she was looking for.

Three months later Nora's mother died, with Nora by her side. After the funeral, sorting through her mother's affairs, Nora saw several bottles of the antibiotics over which they had had the row. 'Why was I so stupid to stick to my guns at that stage? Why?' she wondered. It then dawned on her that the pills, the silverware and the missing key had served a useful function, providing her mother with a much-needed diversion that evening; that her mother's preoccupation with these things must have reflected but also alleviated her anxiety about Nora's leaving. From that perspective, Nora judged her mother to have been much braver than she had given her credit for, that one awful evening.

Egyptians Who Cannot
Fill in a Form in Arabic

It was quite a scene in front of the *Mugama* that morning.
Hundreds of men and women clustered in loosely formed
lines, some accompanied by children, were standing, sitting on
stools and folding chairs, drinking, eating or reading the morning
news in front of the massive fourteen-storey, ugly government
building, erected at the end of the monarchy and the butt of
countless jokes since.

It was not yet eight in the morning. The men and women
had roused themselves at the crack of dawn to make it to the
Mugama so early for the same reason, to apply for an exit visa. The
government was issuing exit visas to Egyptians wishing to travel
abroad. No visa, no travel! Visas were issued only intermittently.
There was no way of knowing when the door to the outside
world would slam shut again. Leaving the country was a difficult
affair for Egyptians in those days. Adequate letters of invitation
from friends or relatives abroad had to be provided – letters in
which the friends or relatives promised to support the applicant,

as travellers would be permitted to take only a nominal sum of money out of the country. And, if the visa materialised, air travel would have to be on Egyptair.

Some of these people were not even certain that they would actually be travelling. But that did not seem to matter. They wanted the freedom that the visa represented. And they had come fully prepared to wait for hours, to elbow their way into the building, to run from one office to the next in search of stamps, signatures and seals, and, once all this was done, to struggle out of the building, with the visa in hand – or almost in hand.

Amongst them there were well-to-do Egyptians whose economic assets were under assault from the new regime – Egyptians who, in the eyes of the country's new leaders, were suspect for being too enmeshed in the old order, or not Egyptian enough.

In a sense, the country's new leaders were correct. There were certainly those in the crowd waiting in front of the *Mugama* that morning who were imbued with a sense of superiority by virtue of their social background and considered themselves as a cut above ordinary Egyptians; and those who, from the outset, had only contempt for the new leaders; and those who had turned bitter because they felt dispossessed even of their Egyptianness, as their loyalty and commitment to the country came under attack daily from the new leaders

One of the first to arrive in front of the *Mugama* the day so many Egyptians flocked to its doors in the hope of obtaining an exit visa was Mrs T., a slight, middle-aged woman with a parasol in hand – a vestige of this old order that the new one was so keen on dismantling. Though without a shred of old regime elitism, this lady stood out, paradoxically, as a caricature of the much-decried old order and its Western orientation. She was an Egyptian who had lived all her life in the country yet spoke its language very poorly, and could neither read it nor write it – one of those Egyptians who spoke virtually only French, thought and felt only in French; an Egyptian who, by the standards of the new regime, did not belong in the country. Of that Mrs T. herself needed no convincing. She was quite aware that people like her had become anachronistic in post-1952 Egypt. She also knew that the old order of things had been both unfair and unsustainable; so she was not altogether opposed to the changes that the country was undergoing. She had that rare quality of being open-eyed about the world she belonged to – as open-eyed as one can be when change is about to engulf one's world. Her lucidity, sometimes but not always a blessing, did not make life any easier for her, as it intensified her sense that the new Egypt taking shape was leaving her in an untenable situation.

Anxious by nature, Mrs T. was full of big and small anxieties the morning she arrived at the *Mugama* so early. Her chief concern had to do with a major issue hanging over her. She was at difficult crossroads. Were she to get the magic visa, she could start her life afresh in Geneva, working in a bookstore to be opened soon by a friend of hers. To be offered employment at her age was, she realised, a rare opportunity. But would she have the energy and courage to take that step? It would involve persuading her elderly husband of the wisdom of the move and overcoming his reluctance to become entirely dependent on her. In Geneva her employment would be their only source of income. They had no money abroad, not having had the foresight to get money out of the country before the government's restrictions made it virtually impossible to do so. Leaving her husband behind was a possibility. The marriage had been rocky for years. Twice, on her initiative, they had lived apart for extended periods, at the end of which she had yielded to her husband's entreaties to give the marriage another go. They had no children. This should have made her leaving him relatively easy, but it had not. She was bound to him by compassionate feelings, more so than ever now that he was really getting on in age.

So, to some extent, Mrs T. was afraid of getting the visa: if she did, it would leave her in a quandary. To stay in Egypt seemed senseless to her. But to leave her husband behind would require a callousness she doubted she had. And to persuade him to join her in Geneva, once she had set up house there, would saddle her with a responsibility she did not really wish to assume.

Just before she had stepped out of the apartment that early morning, her husband had come out of his bedroom looking forlorn, and, though he knew the answer, had made a point of asking, 'So, you're going to the *Mugama* to apply for a visa?' Without looking at him, she replied hurriedly, 'Yes, I am! I am!' begrudging him his obvious vulnerability but also feeling sorry for him. A heavy smoker, he had coughed a lot – more than usual it seemed to Mrs T. – and, after his coughing fit, declared feeling out-of-sorts. This made her turn her face away in exasperation only to hear him mutter, 'How could I contemplate travelling anywhere in the condition I'm in?' Watching him shuffle back to his bedroom, Mrs T. forced herself to say, as calmly as she could, 'It's very early. Have some rest. Hopefully, you'll feel better later in the morning,' and rushed out of the door, feeling more apprehensive than ever about the choices she might have to make, should she obtain a visa.

The more immediate reason for Mrs T.'s nervousness that morning was the prospect of having to deal with the *Mugama*'s bureaucracy. Any time she was about to find herself in a situation where her deficiency in Arabic was bound to become evident, she worried that some bureaucrat might quiz her – even if not in an ill-meaning way – about her lamentable Arabic. Her fears had some basis: that was happening more and more often. It usually went this way: 'So you're Egyptian!' the bureaucrats would say, sounding surprised, after looking at her identification papers. 'It must be by marriage!' they would declare, only to exclaim, once they had looked more closely at her documents, 'Your father was Egyptian and you were born here!' Then, some would conclude, 'So you must have lived much of your life abroad!' While others would ask – sometimes innocently but not always so innocently – 'But then tell me why is your Arabic so poor and so foreign-sounding?'

How to begin explaining to them her appalling Arabic? Blame her Syro-Lebanese father's fixation on France, even though the man himself, a journalist, had been as fluent in Arabic as in French? Tell them that, throughout her childhood, her father had heaped French books on French history upon her – never once a book on Egyptian history? Blame it on her mother's Swiss origins? These were not good enough excuses. After all, she had lived all of her life in Egypt, so why hadn't she learnt the language properly, later on in life? Sure, it was a very difficult language. And yes, she was not particularly gifted for languages. Still, she had been remiss. She had done absolutely nothing to lessen her foreignness in her own country, behaving all along as if she thought it was a lost cause – now clearly a self-fulfilling prophecy.

While waiting for the *Mugama* to open, Mrs T. made no attempt at conversation with those around her; nor did she pay any attention to their animated talk. Every so often she would glance at a page or two of the book she had brought along, Marguerite Duras' *Moderato Cantabile*. She didn't try to read properly: she was too nervous for that.

The *Mugama* finally opened its doors slightly after eight and the crowd of impatient applicants thronged the building. Mrs T. was fortunate – she was amongst the first to enter – yet her anxiety did not ease. On the contrary, it became more acute. For a brief moment she thought of turning back, but the swarm of bodies behind her pushed her further inside. 'The die is cast,' she told herself. And, all of a sudden, she was determined to get that visa. She felt that it was imperative for her to decide for herself, visa in hand, whether or not to leave Egypt and give up for good a life she had grown uncomfortable with but was – for better or worse – accustomed to.

Carried by the flow of people, clutching the application forms (completed in Arabic by a cousin), her friend's invitation letter and a letter from her husband authorising her to travel, she forged ahead, walked up the stairs to the first floor, then straight through the *Mugama*'s airless hallways, into room number 52, the first in a series of rooms abuzz with government employees processing the applications through all the different steps required.

In anticipation of the deluge of applicants, the employees in room 52 – except for one cheerful-looking young man – exuded a harassed air. Whether it was their customary morning ritual or whether it was to soothe their already frayed nerves, the employees – all five of them, including the cheerful-looking one – were drinking tea or coffee. Spotting the one with the cheerful face, Mrs T. tried to attract his attention, but to no avail, for he was telling some joke to his colleagues. So she ended up giving her documents to a dour young man who took the documents, yawned widely and, noticing the parasol in her hand, remarked casually, 'So you don't much like the sun?'

Set on saying as little as possible, Mrs T. answered, 'Not very much.'

'Why?' the young man asked while studying her application. 'The sun is nice, very nice.'

She did not answer.

He yawned again and started discussing loudly some business matter from the previous day with a colleague standing at the opposite side of the room. It was getting hot in the room, by now so full that one could hardly move in and out of it. 'We need fans,' said the dour-looking young employee while perusing, once again, Mrs T.'s application.

To stop more people from trying to come in, a large woman, sitting at the one and only desk in the room, yelled at a small and sprightly older man whose main task seemed to be serving tea and coffee, to close the door. Loud protests from the hallway were heard as the door was shut.

While this was going on, Mrs T. noticed with alarm that the young man studying her documents was frowning and shaking his head.

'Anything wrong?' she asked, visibly worried.

'There's a problem,' he said, more gently than she would have expected. 'Your application is incomplete. You needed to fill in another form.'

'What form?' Mrs T. asked with a sinking heart.

'I'll get it for you,' the young man offered with as much grace as one could hope for in the circumstances.

Mrs T. took comfort from the young man's softer tone. He disappeared, reappearing a couple of minutes later with a form that he handed to Mrs T. Despite the chaotic atmosphere in the room, things seemed to get done somehow.

'There it is,' he said somewhat nonchalantly. 'I'll let you fill it in, then give it back to me.' Before she had mustered the courage to ask for his help, he looked at her and asked bluntly, 'But can you actually fill it in? You sound like one of those Egyptians who might not be able to!'

'Can you help me?' she said almost in a whisper.

Pointing to the people standing in the room, he answered, 'I would on a normal day, but you can see for yourself how busy we are.' Then he added, 'You should learn Arabic, to read it and write it. It's never too late. I'm sure you could.'

Standing nearby, the cheerful-looking employee had apparently overheard the conversation and butted in: 'Why don't you ask him to teach you? He's a graduate in linguistics. He graduated with honours,' he told Mrs T. The suggestion brought a smile to his colleague's face.

Suddenly, the woman sitting at the desk – evidently some sort of supervisor – was heard screaming, 'Enough, you people! Enough chit-chat! There's no time for that!'

Undaunted, the cheerful young employee retorted, 'But the lady needs help. She can't fill in the form.'

'We're too busy to help her, or to help anyone, for that matter,' the woman shouted. Then she was heard mumbling, 'God, give me patience! Egyptians who can't read and write Arabic, who can't even fill in a simple application form in Arabic!'

A couple of applicants muttered something that sounded as if they were commiserating, though it was not clear with whom exactly. Others were heard saying, 'It's time for work, not useless talk.'

Mortified and seething with anger, but also full of shame, Mrs T. pretended that she had heard nothing.

'But the lady is not to be blamed,' the morose-looking employee suddenly said to everybody and anybody. 'The olden days are to be blamed!' Then, to Mrs T. herself, who was still standing behind the counter and hoping against hope that some help would be offered, he said, 'I would like to help you but, as you can see, the supervisor's getting all steamed up. Who knows, you might be lucky and find someone in the hallway willing to lend you a hand. If not, come back tomorrow. God willing, I'll be here, though the way things are going, I'll probably be ill in bed.'

Mrs T. thanked him, collected her documents and manoeuvred her way through room 52 – without her parasol.

When, later in the day, the jovial employee saw the parasol leaning against the counter, he announced, 'It must belong to the lady who had problems filling in her form.' And his bossy supervisor shot back, 'Can't fill in a form in Arabic and can't tolerate the sun! What is she doing in the country?' To which the young man said, jokingly, 'Well then, you should have let us fill in the forms for her.'

Once in the hallway, it didn't take long for Mrs T. to realise that asking for help was out of the question; people were too preoccupied. All that was left for her to do was to force her way through the crowd, along the hallways, down the stairs and into the square, where, sighing a sigh of relief mixed with disappointment, she breathed in all the fresh air she could. Feeling the sun on her face, she noticed that she had left her parasol in room 52. And she immediately took this as a sign – the sign that, no matter what, she must return to the *Mugama*, endure the wait and the crowds, face the bureaucrats, get her visa and her parasol back. No matter what!

She hurried back home, obsessing over the form that needed to be completed. Who would fill it in for her? Might her husband be willing to do it, if her cousin was not available? It was past nine. To return to the *Mugama* later in the day would be pointless. She would never make it into room 52, judging by the size of the crowd still waiting outside. She would return to the *Mugama* tomorrow. She would make sure to be there even earlier than she had been that morning.

As soon as she stepped into her apartment, the maid, part of the household for over twenty years, came running to the door, screaming, 'Thank God, you're back early! Thank God! The master's been taken ill! Very ill! The doctor is in his room right now.'

No sooner had the maid finished saying this, than Mrs T.'s sister-in-law walked into the hall where Mrs T. and the maid were still standing. 'He had a stroke,' the sister-in-law declared accusingly. 'Just like that! Soon after you left this morning!' Then, her sister-in-law asked Mrs T. with unconcealed bitterness, 'And did you get that visa?'

The question triggered very unpleasant feelings in Mrs T, who heard herself burst out, 'What does it matter if I did? I couldn't leave now anyway, could I?' It stunned her that she should be capable of such a harsh answer. She took a deep breath and closed her eyes.

Though not understanding the meaning of the exchange, spoken in French, the maid sensed the tension between the two women and, trying to calm things down, she urged Mrs T., 'Don't get so upset, things will be alright. God is with you.'

Mrs T. walked towards her husband's bedroom with the maid beside her. Her sister-in-law held back for a few seconds, then followed them in.

Glossary

Galabeyah	robe-like outer garment
Khamsin	hot sand-laden wind blowing in from the desert
Khan El Khalili	large souk in Islamic Cairo
Khawaga	a Westerner or someone perceived as a Westerner
Mugama	a building on Midan El Tahrir ('Liberation Square') in which a wide range of governmental services are provided
Mukwagi	clothes ironer
Olla	clay water jar
Thanawiya	Secondary Certificate School Examination